HE WAS GOING ... TO KILL HIM. IT WAS JUST A MATTER OF TIME.

The sand was everywhere, filling Cole's eyes, his nose, his mouth, and his ears. Working its way into his clothes to scrape against his skin. It was above him, and below him. There before him, and following after him. Wrapping itself around him like a long-lost sweetheart. Claiming him, at last, for its very own.

Cole could feel his heart beating hard and fast. Though the sand muffled the sound, there was a ringing in his ears. Dimly, he realized it emanated from his own body, from his head, and his desperately aching lungs.

He tried struggling against the hands that held him, forcing him through the sand like a worm through dirt, but he knew it was useless. His strength was failing. He was weak. They were strong. And there were so very, very many of them.

Charmed®

Published by Simon & Schuster

Charmed ®

TRUTH AND CONSEQUENCES

An original novel by Cameron Dokey

Based on the hit TV series created by

Constance M. Burge

SIMON PULSE

New York London Toronto Sydney Singapore

First Simon Pulse edition November 2003

® & © 2000 Spelling Television Inc. All rights reserved.

SIMON PULSE
An imprint of Simon & Schuster
Children's Publishing Division
1230 Avenue of the Americas
New York, NY 10020

Printed in the United States of America

10 9 8 7 6 5 4 3 2 1

Library of Congress Control Number 2003108967

ISBN 0-689-85791-8

TRUTH AND
CONSEQUENCES

Prologue

It was a dark and foggy night.

Thick, stealthy, penetrating fog. The kind of fog that slithers down alleys, pokes its fingers down chimneys, gathers in streets, piling up upon itself until it forms solid walls.

All over San Francisco, lights winked out as the fog crept in and swallowed them up. Familiar landmarks dissolved. Familiar faces metamorphosed into strangers, features obscured and altered by the mist. The thicker the fog became, the more reality became an abstract concept. Illusion ruled the day.

And the night.

Even San Franciscans born and bred, the ones most accustomed to the way the white stuff rolled off the bay at nightfall, folded their arms across their chests and shivered. In every neighborhood, people cut short meetings or errands after work, eager to be home, safe and sound.

And there was a thought no one quite dared to voice aloud. Because they couldn't quite believe they were actually thinking it. A creep-out thought of astronomic proportions. Telling themselves they were imagining things didn't do any good. Neither did wondering whether they'd watched one too many episodes of *The Twilight Zone*.

Because even as San Franciscans tried to talk themselves out of it, the thought remained:

Something was coming. Something that didn't belong. Something you definitely did not want to meet in person.

It was coming with the fog.

From across the street, he watched them. The three witches. The Charmed Ones. Collective thorn in the side of all things dark and dangerous.

He was one of them.

He'd heard of the Charmed Ones before, of course. Few things in the underworld hadn't. But he had his own agenda, his own needs, his own mission. And they hadn't brought him into direct contact with the world's most powerful witches. Until now, the Charmed Ones simply hadn't interested him.

All that had changed tonight.

Doing recon wasn't really necessary. There was no actual need for him to be standing on a dank, cold San Francisco street, staring at a brightly lit house. But he was curious, he had to admit. Just who were they, these women who were so much more than their surface images? These Charmed Ones.

In a strange way, he felt a sort of kinship, he supposed. He, too, was much more than he seemed, and none of it good. A thing that made him their opposite.

He crossed the street and walked boldly through the front yard. Right up to the front window. He knew he didn't have to worry that he might be spotted. No one could see him unless he wished to be seen. And he didn't. Not yet. That time was yet to come.

So he contented himself with watching as the witches moved through the rooms of their house, his eyes seeing in a way no normal mortal could. But then, there wasn't much point in comparing him with what was normal. Of his own free will, he'd stopped being what other men were a very, very long time ago.

One of the Charmed Ones was setting the table for dinner; another chopped veggies for a salad. The third was stirring something that steamed gently on top of the stove. They looked domestic. Safe. Content.

Enjoy it while you can, witches, he thought. And his face lit in an unholy smile. As he watched, the one making salad finished her task and began to move through the house. Closing shutters, pulling drapes. Blocking out the night, the fog. When she reached the front window, she paused.

Her hand hesitated on the window sash. He could have sworn he heard her catch her breath, and he almost laughed in delight. So this one was spooked by the entrance he'd chosen. Made uneasy by the fog.

He caused a great wave to surge up around the window with a wave of one hand.

You like my entrance? he inquired silently as the fog swirled around him, concealing as a magician's cloak. *Wait till you see what I do for an encore.*

And then, as silently and invisibly as he had come, the watcher in the night was gone.

"Phoebe?" said Piper Halliwell's quiet voice. "Is something wrong?"

Standing by the front window, Phoebe Halliwell started. *What on earth is the matter with me?* she thought. Ever since the fog had started to roll in, she'd been nervous and edgy. Glancing over her shoulder as if expecting to find someone behind her, only to discover each and every time she did so that there was no one there.

Of course.

She hadn't even realized she'd been doing it until she'd caught both her sisters glancing at her with concern. After that, she'd controlled herself. But the feeling hadn't gone away. If anything, it had only gotten worse. Finally, Phoebe couldn't stand it any longer.

Maybe if I close the drapes, she thought. Maybe then she'd finally be able to rid herself of the notion that there was something out there. In it. Waiting and watching.

She'd almost convinced herself she'd done it, until she'd reached to close the living room shades and felt . . . what was it? Not a premonition. It wasn't that specific. Just a feeling. More than a feeling, a certainty now.

There was something in the fog. Something that wasn't right.

And, if past history was anything to go by, chances were good that, sooner or later, it would do what things-that-weren't-quite-right always did.

It would make its presence known to the Charmed Ones.

Chapter

1

Two days later, all traces of the fog had vanished, and San Francisco was back to normal. All over the city, people were out on the town, even though it was still the middle of the week.

It was Wednesday night, and Phoebe Halliwell was all dressed up with someplace to go.

She was already there, in fact. "There" being San Francisco's hottest new romantic date spot, a chic little French bistro called Chez Richard. The look Phoebe had chosen for the evening was as hot as her location. Even if, at the moment, she was the only one around to say so herself.

She'd found the dress just yesterday, at her favorite boutique. On sale, no less. An event that had done a fair amount to dispel her lingering feelings of weirdness about the fog. The dress was silk, the color of ripe cherries, the perfect complement to Phoebe's dark hair and eyes.

Cut in a way that tantalized yet never revealed.

It must have something to do with the fact that I'm about to become "the little woman," Phoebe thought wryly. *All of a sudden I'm looking for a little mystery in my relationship-life.*

Not that the lack of it had ever really been a problem.

The look and the location could be considered the good points about the evening. The bad point would be that, so far, Phoebe was the only one around to appreciate the good points. Her fiancé, Cole Turner, was late, and Phoebe had no idea why.

Cole, where are you? she wondered.

She shifted on her tiny bar stool, feeling the way the silk *swooshed* against her legs as she uncrossed, then recrossed them. *I wonder if this counts as aerobic exercise,* she thought. If so, she'd already worked off whatever dinner she might order, even if it included one of the cream-filled pastries for which Chez Richard was so renowned. Phoebe snuck a quick look at her watch. By her estimation, she'd been uncrossing and recrossing her legs for at least twenty minutes.

Get a grip, she silently remonstrated as she performed her leg exercise one more time. *So Cole's a little late. Traffic's bad.* Phoebe had encountered that phenomenon herself on the way to the restaurant. Come to think of it, she couldn't remember the last time she'd seen so many people out on a Wednesday night. The tiny restaurant was jammed even though it was only the middle of the week.

Maybe Cole's caught in some guys-operate-in-a-different-time-zone-loop, she hypothesized to herself. Cole *was* completely mortal now, after all. Maybe running late was some weird mortal-guy-initiation-type-thing.

And maybe not.

Phoebe took a swig of the mineral water she'd ordered, wincing as the tiny bubbles burned their way down her throat. She knew better than to let herself believe that the fact that things had been quiet on the disgusting-underworld-thugs-determined-to-kill-the-man-she-loved-no-matter-what front lately meant that Cole's former associates had stopped hunting him.

Demons just weren't all that big on letting bygones be bygones.

If anything, the fact that things had been quiet on the attack front could be considered a bad sign. After all, the action had to start up again sometime. And there was no denying that Cole had some major enemies of the big, bad supernatural kind. Just as there was no denying the fact that his love for Phoebe was a major part of how he'd acquired them.

Although it might be true that all guys had the potential to harbor a secret inner dark side, Cole's had actually had a name. He'd literally been half human, half demon, and his inner dark side had been a red-and-black being called Belthazor.

The demon Belthazor had had a mission: Destroy Phoebe and her older sisters, Prue and Piper, who, together, just happened to be the world's most powerful witches, the Charmed Ones.

Everything had been going pretty well for Belthazor's plan, until Cole, his human side, had done something totally unexpected. He'd fallen in love with one of his intended victims. With Phoebe, to be precise. As fate would have it, Phoebe returned Cole's love. Together, they'd vanquished Belthazor, and now Cole was completely human.

But their happiness had come with a price. . . .

Prue, Phoebe thought as an image of her lost sister swam unexpectedly into her mind. Phoebe blinked rapidly, struggling against the sudden hot prick of tears at the back of her eyes, willing them not to fall.

It did no good to weep for Prue. She was gone. It was both as simple and as complicated as that. And Phoebe had the feeling her oldest sister would be both touched and frustrated by her tears. *You know I love you, Phoebes*, she could practically hear Prue say in her slightly raspy voice, *but I fulfilled my destiny, while yours is still in front of you. You have* got *to move on.*

I know, Phoebe thought. *I know, Prue. It's just . . .*

Just that moving on was a whole lot easier said than done. It still hurt Phoebe to think of her oldest sister. Prue had given her life protecting the innocent, performing the duty of the Charmed Ones.

And, with her death, the Power of Three had been broken. For a while, in spite of Cole and Phoebe's love, it had looked as if Belthazor and the powers of darkness would triumph. But it was then that the miracle—or at the very least, the unexpected—had arrived in the form of Paige Matthews.

Paige, whom Phoebe and Piper had initially believed was an innocent needing their protection, even if they weren't sure that they *could* protect anyone anymore. Paige, who'd been drawn to the Halliwell sisters for reasons she couldn't explain, and wasn't really all that sure she wanted to.

But, in the end, it had been those very reasons that had set them all on the path to healing . . . had given Paige the pieces of herself she'd always sensed were missing . . . had given Phoebe and Piper back a sister. Made the Power of Three possible once more.

Paige's last name might be Matthews, but in several ways that seriously counted, she was most definitely a Halliwell.

She was Phoebe and Piper's half sister, to be exact. The daughter their mother had sought to protect by giving her up for adoption. The child of a forbidden love between a witch and the Whitelighter sent to watch over her.

I guess unusual love stories sort of run in the family, Phoebe mused. As if she and Cole weren't enough, there was her sister Piper and Piper's husband, Leo, who was the Charmed Ones' own Whitelighter. Their love had been put to the test more times than Phoebe could count. But their commitment to each other had finally won over even Leo's bosses, the Council of Elders. Unlike her mother, Piper had been able to marry her Whitelighter.

Which explained why none of the Halliwell girls had known about Paige, even though she was their half sister. Though initially hesitant— okay, make that totally freaked—about her new situation, Paige had eventually been won over. She'd embraced her powers, her duty, her destiny. The Power of Three, the circle of the Charmed Ones, had been restored.

Life sure can be surprising sometimes, Phoebe thought. And not all of the surprises were of the big-ick kind. Discovering Paige had been kind of amazing, particularly as it meant Phoebe wasn't the youngest anymore. She was the middle sister now, a position that had definitely given her a new appreciation for Piper, who, with Prue's death, had become the oldest of the Charmed Ones.

Piper had always been the mediator, the one who kept peace between organized Prue and free-spirited Phoebe. Now, it was Phoebe who tried to keep things on an even keel between risk-taking Paige and the I'm-the-oldest-now-so-I-have-to-be-more-cautious Piper. It hadn't been easy for any of them at first, but, lately, it had seemed to Phoebe that things were getting better between the oldest and the youngest. Piper and Paige had certainly been spending more time together. Giggling and whispering, just like they'd been pals forever. They'd been getting along so well, in fact, there were moments their new behavior sometimes took Phoebe completely by surprise.

Maybe that's *why Cole's late*, Phoebe thought suddenly, her mind making a strange word association with the word *surprise*. She'd come to believe some of the weird leaps her mind made were linked to her powers of premonition. Her ability to see things other people couldn't.

Hey, it was better than thinking she was nuts.

Maybe Cole was late because he'd stopped along the way to cook up some surprise for her, like picking out a bunch of her favorite flowers. Cole had been as excited about their big night out as Phoebe was. Stopping for a surprise was exactly the sort of thing he would do, now that he was trying so hard to succeed at being a mortal. He might not stop to consider it would make him late.

That has to be it, Phoebe thought as she felt the

tension begin to ease from her shoulders. Cole's lateness was the result of some extra treat he'd planned for her. It had absolutely nothing to do with any supernatural changes. She was over-reacting, a thing she had to admit she was prone to do. She should just get over it, relax, and enjoy herself.

As if on cue, her cell phone wailed like a ban-shee. Phoebe jumped so violently, she almost tumbled right off her bar stool. *I have* got *to get some catchy tune for that thing,* she thought as she fumbled to open the clasp of an evening purse not much bigger than the cell itself. "Hello?"

"Phoebe?"

Phoebe slumped over, resting her elbows on the bar as relief swept through her. *"Cole."*

"Hey," Cole said, and Phoebe thought she detected a note of concern in his voice. "I'm sorry I'm not there yet, but I can explain. Are you all right?"

"Of course I'm all right," Phoebe said. "The question is, are you?"

"Why wouldn't I be all right?" Cole asked. There was a tiny pause. "Okay, scratch that," he amended after a moment. "Look, Phoebe—"

"You're sure," Phoebe interrupted. She knew she was sounding slightly hysterical, but she just couldn't seem to help herself. She *had* been wor-ried, in spite of her best efforts to the contrary. "Your voice sounds kind of, I don't know, funny." Visions of Cole trapped in some terrible underworld cave, pinned down by demons, swam through her mind.

"Phoebe, honey," Cole said, his voice patient. "I'm on a cell phone."

Phoebe pulled in a breath. *Come on, Halliwell. Keep it together. Don't go to pieces now.* "Point taken," she acknowledged. *For crying out loud,* she thought. *When did I become Little Miss Clinging Vine?*

If this was what being engaged did to a girl, maybe she and Cole should reconsider tying the knot. Phoebe'd always prided herself on her independence. This kind of behavior wasn't like her at all. "Cole."

"Yes?" Cole said.

"Will you please just tell me where you are?"

"I'm at the office," Cole answered immediately. "I'm sorry I didn't phone sooner, but I've been tied up."

"Just so long as you don't mean literally," Phoebe said as she felt her fear deflate like a pricked balloon.

How much more of an idiot can I possibly be? she wondered. Not one of the scenarios for disaster she'd conjured up to explain Cole's absence had included the one most women would consider obvious: that her sweetie had simply been held up at the office.

"Fortunately, no," Cole replied. "But I'm afraid that's as good as the news gets. I'm sorry, Phoebe, but I—" He broke off, as if uncertain how to continue.

"You're not going to be able to make it tonight," Phoebe filled in for him.

"No, I'm not," Cole admitted at once, sounding relieved that she was taking it well. "It's this big murder case," he hurried on. Cole was an assistant district attorney. Originally, it had been his cover, his way to get to the Charmed Ones. Now, though, it was a job he valued. A way for him to take an active role in righting wrongs.

"Something completely unexpected has literally just come to our attention," Cole went on. "I can't go into details, but . . . it's new information. Information that could blow our case apart. I can't leave now. None of the team can. Not until we get this sorted out. I'm sorry. I know this was supposed to be our special evening, but I—"

"Cole," Phoebe interrupted, her tone firm but gentle. Now that she knew what the situation was, that Cole was safe, she was on solid ground. "I understand. It's all right. If there's one thing you don't have to explain to me, it's that work has to come first sometimes."

"You are one in a million, you know that, don't you?" Cole said, after a brief pause.

"Just one in three," Phoebe answered. "Those odds are good enough for me."

"Why don't you call your sisters?" Cole suggested.

"Get real!" Phoebe said with a laugh, even as she privately acknowledged it was a good thought. "You don't seriously mean to suggest Paige is free."

"Of course not. What was I thinking?" Cole came back. "But what about—" His voice cut off, and Phoebe heard a murmur of voices in the background. "I'm sorry, Phoebe," Cole said after a moment. "Break time's over. Looks like I have to go. I'll be home just as soon as I can, okay?"

"Okay," Phoebe said. "I love you, Cole."

"Yeah, um, thanks," Cole said. "What I mean is—"

"Cole."

"Yes, Phoebe."

"Just say, 'Same to you, but more of it.'"

"Same to you, but more of it," Cole repeated obligingly. A moment later, one of his rare chuckles sounded through the phone. "Did I just do what I think I did?" he asked.

"You absolutely did," Phoebe replied. "And the best part is, you and I are the only ones who know."

So he felt he couldn't say "I love you" with his colleagues in the room. Cole was getting more mortal by the moment. No two ways about it.

"I could get used to this being mortal thing," Cole commented in a lowered voice, as if he'd read her mind.

"I'm counting on it," Phoebe said. "See you at home."

"Right," Cole affirmed. He terminated the connection. Phoebe did the same, then sat for a moment, gazing down at her cell phone.

She'd just been stood up by the love of her life at the most romantic date spot in town. And what was she doing?

Grinning like a fool at her cell phone.

Phoebe was laughing as she punched in the number for home.

Chapter

2

Now that's *what I call . . . odd.*

Phoebe turned off the cell phone and returned it to her purse. A tiny frown snaked down between her eyebrows. Her lips no longer curved in a smile. Her situation-not-quite-normal intuition was working again—this time, as a result of her phone call. Something was definitely up at home, not that she'd actually gotten confirmation of that from Piper or Paige.

She'd invited her sisters to join her for dinner. Both had turned her down.

Paige had been the first to decline Phoebe's invitation. Phoebe had been so surprised, she was pretty sure her jaw had actually dropped open. Paige Matthews turn down an invitation to slip into some glad rags to go out on the town? Since when?

When Phoebe had blurted out the first thing

that came to mind—something along the lines of, *Paige, are you sure you feel all right?*—Paige had simply laughed and reminded her next oldest sister that even the most devoted party girls need to stay home and recharge the batteries once in a while. Besides, spend the evening at the newest romantic hot spot in town with her *sister*?

Paige Matthews thought not.

She has a point, Phoebe thought as she glanced at the mirror over the bar and allowed her gaze to sweep over the cozy restaurant. With the exception of the guy on the equally tiny bar stool just to her right, Phoebe was the only single in the place.

After Paige had declined, naturally Phoebe had tried Piper. She'd even gone so far as to make the supreme sacrifice and offer her dinner reservation to Piper and Leo. But, to her continued astonishment, Piper'd said *no* too. On both counts. While it was true she was taking a rare night off from her nightclub, P3, Leo was out, performing some mysterious spur-of-the-moment task for the Elders. That ruled out a date night for them.

But Piper didn't feel she could abandon Paige. They'd already agreed to settle in for an evening of chick-flick video watching. When Phoebe had phoned, Piper'd been in the kitchen, assembling the ingredients for her secret recipe gourmet popcorn.

Nobody seems to care about abandoning me, Phoebe thought glumly. She knew her sisters hadn't done it on purpose, but hearing about what a swell evening they were going to have without her did make her feel a little left out.

Phoebe tightened her grip on her glass of mineral water. She'd weathered Cole's news that he'd been held up at the office just fine. It was the thought of her sisters having a good time without her that had her all bummed.

"I understand," said a loud voice beside her. Phoebe jerked, startled, and sent a wave of mineral water sloshing onto the bartop. It headed for the sleeve of the guy sitting just to the right of her, foaming across the counter like a tsunami. Phoebe made a sound of dismay, and the guy turned toward her, eyes growing wide as he realized what was happening. He whipped his arm out of the way in the nick of time.

"Of *course* I really mean it," he said. Now that he was facing her, Phoebe could see that, just as she had been, he was talking on a cell phone. "These things happen. I know you can't predict—I'll call you tomorrow—*what?*"

His voice grew progressively more strained, striving to remain good-natured and understanding. *Uh-oh,* Phoebe thought. She knew that tone of voice. It gave her a pretty good indication of what was happening on the other end of the call.

"Out of town. I see," the guy went on. With his free hand, he signaled to the bartender, indicating the puddle of spilled water. "You forgot before, but you just remembered now. No, no, I understand perfectly. Have a good trip. I'll touch base when you get back."

Or not, Phoebe thought, before she could help herself. Even one sided, she knew a brush-off when she heard one.

The bartender arrived, soaking up Phoebe's spilled drink with an immaculate white towel. Phoebe used his appearance as an excuse to shift position slightly, angling away from the guy on the cell phone. She hadn't meant to eavesdrop on what was obviously a painful conversation. All she'd wanted was to keep his sleeve from getting soaked.

"Would *Madame* care for another drink?" the bartender inquired.

"*Mademoiselle,*" Phoebe corrected. She knew that much French, at least. No matter what the language, nobody was calling her a *Mrs.* before she was one. "Thank you, but I—"

"Excuse me," the guy beside her interrupted softly, and Phoebe realized his cell phone call was over. "I'd like to buy you a drink, if you'll let me. To say I'm sorry. I think I was the reason you spilled your last one. I didn't mean to startle you. It was the phone call. It . . . I . . . ."

His voice trailed off. Phoebe turned back toward him, and found herself looking into what had to be the world's most gorgeous pair of bright green eyes. Their expression was apologetic, appealing, and ever so slightly sad. Hopeful and world-weary all at once.

Poet's eyes, Phoebe suddenly thought. Set in a face that was pure boy-next-door. Open and earnest. Though the lighting in the restaurant was dim, Phoebe swore she caught a smattering of freckles across the bridge of his nose. His dark hair was long enough to brush his shirt collar. It all made for a combination that packed a surprising punch. *Whoever that woman is, she ought to have her head examined*, Phoebe thought.

"That's all right," she said, her own voice warm. "I got kind of lost in my own thoughts there for a minute. I forgot there were other people around. It was only mineral water."

The guy beside her grinned as if she'd offered him a birthday present. "Mine too," he said, and he lifted his glass to show her. He nodded at the bartender, who whisked away. "Not that I don't enjoy a good glass of wine," he went on. From another guy, the remark would have seemed pretentious. Coming from him, it seemed natural, as if he was sharing a confidence.

"I mean, it seemed rude to drink before my date—"

Abruptly, his face colored, and he broke off.

"You, too, huh?" Phoebe asked, the words out of her mouth before she quite realized they were even in her mind.

He stared, as if really seeing Phoebe for the

very first time. "You're joking," he said simply, after a moment.

Phoebe felt a sudden burst of warmth. *How does he do that?* she wondered. Utter in all sincerity a statement that would sound like a sleazy line coming from anyone else. From him, it sounded like a compliment.

"Trust me," she said. "This is not a thing *any* woman jokes about. My date has to work late, what about yours?"

He gave a snort. "She has to stay home and pack. She 'suddenly' remembered an urgent trip out of town."

Phoebe winced. As excuses went, it *was* pretty lame. So obviously lame, it was impossible not to get the more-than-hint. "Ouch."

He grinned without mirth. "You got that in one." He hesitated, as if holding some internal debate. "You seem to be handling the rejection pretty well."

"That's because it isn't really rejection," Phoebe began. Horrified, she caught herself in the nick of time. What on earth had she been about to say?

Her companion waited until the bartender finished depositing a frosty glass of mineral water in front of each of them before he answered:

"I think the word you're looking for is *dumped*. Not to worry. I do have some prior

experience in these matters, so I know how to
handle myself."

Phoebe could hear the pain beneath his flip-
pant words. "I'm sorry," she said quietly.

"No, I'm the one who's sorry," the guy beside
her said. "How about if we just wipe the slate
clean and start again? Allow me to introduce
myself. I'm Nick Gerrard."

He extended one hand. Phoebe shook it. The
touch of Nick's skin to hers made her palm tingle
ever so slightly. In her single days, she'd have
taken that as a sign of a connection. Now she was
content to ignore it. "Phoebe Halliwell."

"A thousand pardons, Monsieur Gerrard . . ."
The maître d', dressed in an immaculate tuxedo,
had materialized behind Nick's shoulder like a
puff of smoke. Seeing Phoebe's hand in Nick's,
he smiled with obvious delight, believing the
restaurant was working its spell.

"Your table is ready," the maître d' announced.
"If you and the young lady would care to follow
me?" He made a gesture of invitation and
sketched a tiny bow.

Phoebe snatched her hand away. "Oh, but . . . ,"
she sputtered.

"Oh, but that's perfect!" Nick Gerrard
exclaimed suddenly, his eyes somehow manag-
ing to dance with laughter and plead with
Phoebe all at the same time. "Have dinner with
me, Phoebe Halliwell. Don't think. Just say yes."

Phoebe took a breath, to decline, then paused.

Why shouldn't she say yes? Sure, the sensible thing might be to have dinner alone, or call it a night and head for home and the sisterly chick-flick fest. But now that she was facing them head-on, Phoebe had to admit neither of those options had much appeal.

What if she didn't want to do the sensible thing? What if she wanted to have dinner with Nick Gerrard?

The fact that they'd both ended up stranded was pure coincidence, nothing more. After tonight, Phoebe would never see Nick again. They were two strangers, thrown together by circumstance. At the end of the evening, they'd be parted by it.

"Uh-oh," Nick murmured. "I can see by your face what's coming. You're trying to figure out how to let me down easy, but you're still going to say *no*. Don't do it, I'm begging you."

To Phoebe's astonishment, he began to slide from the bar stool as if preparing to kneel at her feet. The maître d' all but clapped his hands in delight.

"Nick Gerrard, don't you dare!" Phoebe somehow choked out. Somewhere in his slide from the bar stool, she'd begun to laugh.

"Just one word will stop me," Nick declared, his eyes dancing wickedly. "Just say it, Phoebe. If you don't, my evening will be a total waste. I found on-street parking."

Phoebe gave up. He really was outrageous. She couldn't remember the last time she'd laughed so hard. "Enough!" she said, raising her hands as if she were a bank teller in a holdup. "I give in. I will have dinner with you. Dutch treat, though, or the deal's off."

This was *not* a date, after all, she reminded herself. The fact that he'd charmed her didn't mean she wouldn't set her own ground rules.

"I have a better idea," Nick said as he straightened up. "I'll treat you, and you treat me. That way, we both get to feel special."

"Agreed," Phoebe said as she slid off her own stool. Then, she couldn't resist an attempt to get the final word in. "I wonder what the most expensive thing on the menu is?"

Chapter

3

"Wait a minute, I left out Janelle," Nick said. "She was a skydiver."

"Don't tell me," Phoebe said as she took a sip of decaf espresso. "She dumped you via skywriting."

"You saw it, didn't you?" Nick moaned, cradling his head in his hands. "I think half of San Francisco did. She had the pilot spell out 'No way, Nick' right over Golden Gate Park."

Phoebe swallowed quickly. It was the only way to avoid choking. Though they'd talked about more mundane matters, too, Nick had spent a good portion of the meal they'd shared regaling her with stories of the various ways in which women had dumped him. Each tale was more fantastic than the last. The fact that Phoebe hadn't believed a word of any of them hadn't made a difference. He'd still made her laugh until her sides hurt.

And it felt good, she realized suddenly. Actually, the whole evening was making her feel good. It wasn't just the fact that she'd laughed harder than she had since Prue died. Having dinner with Nick reminded Phoebe of what it had been like to go out with a friend, of her life before she'd discovered she was one of the Charmed Ones.

Nick had made her the focus of his attention in an entirely platonic way. Asking if the food she'd ordered was to her liking, entertaining her with his ridiculous stories. Encouraging her to tell a few of her own. Trying to get to know her in a way that had never once felt like a come-on. If anything, it was just the opposite.

After that initial handshake, he hadn't touched her. Not once.

Not even a simple hand to the small of the back as the maître d' had guided them across the restaurant. Or a meeting of fingertips as she'd passed him the bread basket or the salt. He'd shown that he respected the boundaries she'd set. That he respected *her*.

I like him, she thought. Too bad he didn't seem quite like Paige's type.

"I want to thank you for this evening, Phoebe," Nick said now, his tone serious as he broke the silence that had fallen between them. "I hope you won't take this the wrong way, but it's been . . . nice."

"That's exactly what I was thinking," Phoebe

said. "And I had a great time too." She lifted her demitasse in a toast. "To nice."

Nick clinked his against it. "To nice." He took a sip of espresso, then set the tiny cup carefully back into its saucer. "Whoever this guy you were supposed to meet is, I hope he appreciates you," he said, without looking up.

"Believe me," Phoebe said quickly as she felt a sudden pang. Had she really gone through the entire meal without talking about Cole? "He does."

She'd been so happy just to relax and let Nick tell his stories. To forget about her own life for a while. Somehow, the subject of the guy Phoebe had been supposed to meet just hadn't come up. Maybe that had been another reason Nick had spun his tall tales. To distract her, by focusing attention on himself.

"He does appreciate me," Phoebe said again. "And, for the record, he's more than just some guy. He's my fiancé, in fact."

Nick looked up. "Your fiancé," he echoed, some expression Phoebe couldn't quite identify coming and going in his eyes. "Congratulations. I hope you'll be very happy."

"We will be," Phoebe said firmly.

"What's his name?"

"His name," said a voice directly above her head, "is Cole."

"Cole!" Phoebe exclaimed as she twisted in her chair to look up at him. In her surprise and delight,

she completely overlooked his tone of voice.
"Sweetie, this is great! You made it after all!"

"Looks that way, doesn't it?" Cole asked softly
as his eyes glowered down into hers. "But maybe
I shouldn't have bothered."

Uh-oh, Phoebe thought. Now that she'd gotten
a good look at Cole, she could see how upset he
was. Though the demon Belthazor had been ban-
ished from Cole, it had been replaced by an old-
fashioned green-eyed monster. It was pretty plain
he'd jumped to the wrong conclusion about the
scene before him.

Cole was jealous. Plain and simple. A good
old human-type mortal emotion.

Phoebe sat up a little straighter in her chair, as
if poked by a pin, as the true meaning of what
was upsetting Cole came home. He'd simply
taken one look and assumed the worst! How
dare he doubt her! If there was one thing Cole
should have known, it was that Phoebe would
never betray him.

She looked up at Cole, matching his glower
with a cold glare. "I think you'd better explain
that last remark."

There was a sudden flurry of movement from
the far side of the table as Nick got to his feet,
plainly determined to head trouble off. "Great
you could make it," he said as he beamed across
the table at Cole. "I'm Nick, by the way—Nick
Gerrard. When Phoebe and I discovered we'd
both ended up sort of unexpectedly on our own

for the evening, we decided to pool our resources. Seemed a shame to waste two perfectly good dinner reservations."

He extended his hand across the table. Cole looked right at him, then thrust his hands into his jacket pockets. Phoebe felt her anger and frustration ratchet up a notch. Cole really was being insufferably rude. She was *not* the prize at the bottom of the Cracker Jack box: something to be fought over by little boys.

"Oh, really," Cole said, his tone plainly showing Nick's attempt to keep things pleasant was going to get him absolutely nowhere. "A shame to waste two perfectly good dinner reservations, so you thought you'd just combine them into one. And whose catchy brainstorm would that have been?"

That's it, Phoebe thought. *I've had enough.*

She got to her feet, causing Cole to back up a step, though he definitely continued to glower. Ignoring him, Phoebe signaled to the waiter, who had begun to hover anxiously. The waves of antagonism were literally rolling off Cole. In a restaurant this small, any change in atmosphere would be noticed by the other diners.

"What difference does it make whose idea it was?" Phoebe asked Cole in an icy voice. "You've obviously made up your mind about what you think happened here this evening. Does it matter which of us actually suggested we have dinner together?"

Cole's jaw clenched. "I think I have a right to know."

Phoebe gave him her deadliest sweet smile. "The same way I have the right to be given the benefit of the doubt, you mean?" she inquired.

The waiter sidled up to the table, clutching the check on a small silver platter. Before Nick could even reach for it, Phoebe snatched it up. "Wait just a moment, please," she instructed the waiter. Sliding the strap of her evening bag from the back of her chair, Phoebe opened her purse and removed her credit card.

"What's going on?" Cole cried. "Don't tell me you're going to buy this guy's dinner!"

"I know we agreed we would share the bill, Nick," Phoebe said, turning to face him across the table, an action that required her to turn her back on Cole. If she'd been more humiliated in public, it sure hadn't been lately. But the fact that Cole was behaving badly didn't mean Phoebe would too. The way she had it figured, she seriously owed Nick Gerrard. He'd made every effort to head off unpleasantness. The fact that he hadn't been successful was not his fault.

"But, under the circumstances, I hope you'll let me pick up the tab," Phoebe went on.

"Phoebe," Nick said, helplessly. "I—"

"Thank you," Phoebe cut him off. She set her credit card and the bill against the silver with a *slap*. "I'll sign the slip at the front desk, if you don't mind," Phoebe told the waiter.

"Hey, lady," the waiter said. "Whatever you want." The possibility of an unpleasant scene had obviously driven all thoughts of the French accent he'd employed earlier in the evening right out of his mind. Plainly grateful to get out of range, the waiter pivoted on one heel and scurried off.

Phoebe slid her evening bag onto her shoulder. She pulled in a silent, steadying breath, then looked straight into Nick Gerrard's eyes. "I want to thank you for a wonderful evening," she said. "I haven't laughed that hard in a very long time. I needed to do some laughing, I think. And I want you to know that I hope . . ." She paused. Behind her, Cole made a dangerous sound. "I hope this evening marks the end of anything even vaguely resembling a skywriting episode."

To her relief, Nick smiled. "That makes two of us," he said softly. "Your fiancé is a very fortunate man," he went on, something hot and dangerous flaring in his eyes as they flicked to Cole. At the expression in them, Phoebe could see the anger Nick had carefully held in check, and felt a second wash of gratitude for him sweep over her. The situation was bad enough just the way it was. But it would have been a whole lot worse if Nick had given in to his anger, the way Cole had.

"I hope he knows it," Nick continued softly as his eyes moved back to Phoebe's, "and that he has the sense to cherish his good fortune. It's been a pleasure to meet you, Phoebe. Good night." Without another word, he cut a wide berth around Cole and walked out of the restaurant.

"Well," Phoebe said, turning back to Cole only when she was sure Nick was gone. "I hope you're proud of yourself." She brushed past Cole and headed for the front of Chez Richard.

"What's that supposed to mean?" Cole snapped as he marched after her. "Wait a minute—let me guess. This is some girl-power thing, isn't it? A way to make me think I'm in the wrong."

Phoebe signed the credit card receipt, wrapped her copy around her card, and slipped them both into her evening bag before she answered. "You *are* in the wrong, Cole."

She pushed open the restaurant doors and stepped out onto the street with a shiver. The fog was back. Great, rolling waves of it swallowing the street like a damp cotton ball.

"Okay, so let me get this straight," Cole said as he followed Phoebe out the door. "I bust my chops to get here at all, and when I do, I find you having dinner with another guy. When I get *understandably* upset about it, suddenly *I'm* the one who's in the wrong? Oh no," Cole said with an emphatic shake of his head. "I don't think so. In fact, I think I'm entitled to an explanation."

"Nick gave you one," Phoebe said. "An

accurate one. You didn't pay much attention, as I recall."

Phoebe could feel the leash she'd been keeping on her own temper begin to fray. She'd been trying to think of how she would have felt if she'd found Cole having dinner with another woman. To put herself in his shoes. But his refusal to so much as listen to reason was making it tough for Phoebe to be reasonable.

"This was supposed to be *our* evening, Phoebe," Cole roared as he stormed after her. "It's not my fault I got held up. I'll bet you didn't even call your sisters, did you?" he asked bitterly. "You just took the first offer that came along."

Phoebe's temper deserted her in an angry red haze. She stopped dead in the middle of the sidewalk. She wasn't cold any longer. In fact, she hardly even noticed the fog. Instead, Phoebe was redhot with anger. Slowly, she turned back to Cole. "How can you say such a thing to me?" she asked, her voice low and intense. "How can you even *think* it, Cole? For your information, I did call my sisters. They were both home and wanted to stay there."

Cole gave a bark of disbelieving laughter. "You expect me to believe Paige wanted to stay home? She never does. You said so yourself."

"Yes, I did say that," Phoebe acknowledged. "But you know what? I was *wrong*. You know about being *wrong*, don't you, Cole? You ought to, because it's what you are, right now. What you've been since you spotted me at that table with Nick and decided it meant I was doing something I shouldn't. And, for the record, I *do* expect you to believe me. Just like I expect something else you seem to have forgotten all about."

"What?" Cole asked. His tone was surly, but Phoebe could tell that her forcefulness was beginning to shake him.

"Trust. I thought I'd earned yours."

"It's not about trust," Cole protested. "It's—"

"It is so," Phoebe shot back. "This is *all* about trust, Cole. And if you can't see that, maybe you're not the man I thought you were."

A horrible silence fell. In it, Cole and Phoebe faced each other on the sidewalk, their breath hanging in the cold, damp air as they each breathed just a little too hard.

"Cut me some slack here, will you?" Cole said at last. His tone was sullen and defensive, like a teenage boy's. "I haven't been one all that long, you know."

"I do know that," Phoebe said. "And I've been trying to take it into account, but I honestly don't think you can use that as an excuse, Cole. Either you trust me, or you don't. It's as simple as that. As far as I'm concerned, this discussion is over. I'm going home now."

Without another word, Phoebe turned and walked to the SUV, leaving Cole standing, open-mouthed, in the middle of the sidewalk.

Chapter

4

The lights of Halliwell Manor gleamed with welcome even through the fog as Phoebe pulled into the driveway. *It feels good to be home*, she thought. She killed the engine, then sat for a moment, resting her forehead on the steering wheel. All of a sudden, she was completely exhausted.

Phoebe had deliberately kept her mind blank, concentrating on the simple act of driving, all the way home from Chez Richard. The fog made it necessary, in the first place. In the second, it was the only way she knew to keep herself from screaming in frustration, or crying in despair. She wasn't quite sure which. Though, sooner or later, she had the feeling it was likely to end up being both.

Better do an image check, she decided as she flipped down the visor and opened the mirror, giving her face a quick once-over in the glow of the overhead dome light. It would never do to go in looking too stressed. Questions from her sisters would be the inevitable result. And much as she knew she'd appreciate their support, Phoebe also knew she wasn't up for explanations. Not yet. Not tonight.

Particularly when all she had were questions of her own.

Such as: If Cole didn't trust her, where did that leave them as a couple?

Don't think about that now, Phoebe counseled herself as she folded up the visor. *Instead, just think positive.* If she did that, chances were good she could make it up to her room before she . . . did whatever it was that she was going to do.

Soaking my head has a certain appeal, she thought as she got out of the car and walked briskly to the front door. She and Cole had been through so much. Surely they'd be able to sort out this all-too-mortal misunderstanding. Still, Cole's lack of faith definitely hurt.

Phoebe put her key into the lock, twisted the front door open, and stepped into the entryway of Halliwell Manor. "Wally, Beaver, I'm home!" she called out.

Silence. *That's odd,* she thought. In the next instant, she could have sworn she heard whispers coming from the general direction of the living room. They were drowned out when the volume on the television suddenly shot up.

"I hate it when she can't remember our names,

don't you?" Paige's voice complained, over the sound.

Still puzzled, Phoebe headed for the living room. Paige was sitting on the couch in an over-sized cotton nightshirt that proclaimed, I ❤ SAN FRANCISCO on the front. Far from her usual style, it had been a gift from a grateful young client of whom she was particularly fond. An enormous bowl of popcorn, so full that some had spilled over the sides, rested on the couch between her and Piper.

Piper was wearing her favorite jammies, the flannels with retro kitchen utensils all over them. She kept her eyes glued to the television set as she reached over to give her youngest sister's knee a pat, then snagged a handful of popcorn.

"Don't take it personally," she recommended with her mouth full.

"The least she can do is call us girls' names," Paige remarked. "And keep your hands off *my* popcorn."

"I'm only eating the ones marked 'Piper,'" Piper said. She tossed another handful into her mouth. Throughout the exchange, neither of her sisters so much as glanced in Phoebe's direction.

So much for worrying that somebody might notice all is not right in my world, Phoebe thought.

One part of her mind knew she ought to feel grateful to be, well, overlooked. Now, she could beat-feet it upstairs before either Paige or Piper realized anything was wrong. Unfortunately for

that part of Phoebe's mind, the other part proclaimed that the fact that her sisters couldn't
even be bothered to look at her had just made
her already-miserable evening even worse.

The least they could do was ask her how
things had gone.

"So, Phoebes," Piper said, her eyes still glued
to the TV screen, "how was your—oh, wow!"
She cut herself off. "This is the best. I absolutely
love this part."

"But it's so sad!" Paige wailed. To Phoebe's
astonishment, Paige's eyes filled with tears. She
put her head down on Piper's shoulder.

"Well, it has to be, silly," Piper consoled Paige
as she gave her head a pat, though her eyes were
beginning to fill, too, Phoebe noticed. "You can't
have a happy ending if you don't go through the
sad stuff first," she sniffled.

"Leave it to you to find the moral of the
story," Paige choked out.

Oh, for crying out loud! Phoebe thought. *What's
gotten into everyone tonight?* Cole was acting like
a jealous husband, and he and Phoebe weren't
even married yet. Paige and Piper were acting
like who-knew-what. Though Phoebe was usually happy to see her brother-in-law, given the
way everyone else had suddenly gone bonkers,
the fact that Leo wasn't around had to be considered a bright spot.

"I'm going up to bed," Phoebe announced.
Not that anyone will notice.

"Sweet dreams, sweetie," Piper bawled.

"See you in the m-m-morning," Paige sobbed.

Phoebe made it as far as the bottom of the stairs before she gave up. "What on earth are you guys watching?"

Paige lifted her head from Piper's shoulder.

"*Raiders of the Lost Ark*."

Cole drove through the night. For reasons he considered obvious, he chose the freeway, not really caring which direction he was going. His car was low-slung and powerful and, even in the always-crowded Bay Area traffic and on a foggy night, he could really open her up. But the faster he drove, the more obvious the truth became:

He had blown it. Big-time.

Phoebe had been pretty clear about the fact that she thought he'd acted like a jealous jerk tonight. Tough as it was for Cole to swallow, the truth was that he'd been in the wrong. Which meant that Phoebe was absolutely right.

On impulse, Cole headed toward Sausalito. For some reason, driving across the Golden Gate Bridge always made him feel better. There was something about the way the great arches of the suspension bridge rose up above him, even as the earth dropped away below.

As he sent the car zooming across the span, Cole wondered how much farther he'd have to drive before he figured out how to perform the action that seemed to be the destiny of mortal men.

Offering an apology to the woman he loved.

Phoebe lay curled in bed, seriously resisting the impulse to pull the covers over her head, an action she usually reserved for her moments of darkest despair. Yes, she was upset, but surely she wasn't *that* far gone tonight.

Was she?

She sat up, punched her bed pillows into submission, then propped herself up against them, leaning against the headboard. Before she completely gave in to the blues, she ought to at least make some attempt to talk herself out of them. If she failed, *then* she could pull the covers over her head, secure in the knowledge that she'd given resisting depression her very best shot.

Phoebe hugged her knees to her chest. *Come on, Halliwell. You can sort this out*, she thought. Between coping with Prue's death and making up her mind about Cole, she'd come to know herself pretty well lately.

All right, let's start with Cole, she told herself. Though his behavior certainly accounted for the lion's share of Phoebe's upset, there was more to what she was feeling than just hurt and dismay over Cole's actions, Phoebe realized suddenly. In fact, the thing that was bothering her most at the moment had nothing to do with Cole. It had to do with Paige and Piper.

Something about the way her sisters were behaving just didn't seem right. *Oh, great*, Phoebe thought. *Now I'm the one who's acting jealous.*

She genuinely wanted Paige and Piper to find more common ground. They were so different. They'd had the hardest time adjusting to the new family togetherness. But wanting them to get along better didn't mean Phoebe wanted to be left out.

And that's just how her sisters' behavior had made her feel, she acknowledged. Unimportant. Excluded. Shut out. Not only that, Piper and Paige's behavior had been so bizarre, Phoebe's sisterly intuition was telling her there had to be some reason for it. There was something her sisters didn't want her to know. That much seemed clear.

The question was, what was it?

Phoebe's knees slipped from her grasp, and her legs shot out straight in front of her as the answer struck her right between the eyes. Now that she'd actually posed the question, the answer seemed blindingly obvious. There was really only one topic her sisters might hesitate to bring up with her: her relationship with Cole. Specifically, their upcoming nuptials.

What if her sisters had decided Cole wasn't right for her after all? What if they'd seen things about him that Phoebe hadn't noticed? Until tonight, that is. When he'd suddenly gone all caveman on her. What if the reason neither Paige nor Piper had been able to meet Phoebe's eyes was because they didn't want her to see the doubt in them?

Phoebe slumped back against the headboard, her hands closing convulsively on her covers as she pulled them up to her chin. Piper had been incredibly supportive of her relationship with Cole, even though he carried an awful lot of baggage along with him. Baggage that could, and had, threatened them all, which was why Paige had been less than enthusiastic about him. What if Paige had changed Piper's mind? What if she was trying to change Phoebe's mind too? The hands clutching the sheets abruptly changed to fists. *But I haven't, have I?*

Don't be ridiculous, Phoebe chided herself as she made a deliberate attempt to relax. Of course she hadn't changed her mind about marrying Cole.

Tonight had been trying, it was true. Phoebe still felt incredibly hurt by the knowledge that Cole's gut reaction had been that he couldn't trust her. But she had to make allowances for the fact that he was still learning to be human. Some of the hard lessons that Phoebe had learned much younger he was just experiencing now. They'd been through so much, come through so many obstacles together, Phoebe couldn't believe they wouldn't come through this one too.

None of which solved the problem of what Paige and Piper were hiding from her.

Phoebe groaned. *All right. That's enough.*

All this soul searching wasn't really getting her anywhere. Instead, it was just encouraging her thoughts to circle, like vultures. There was nothing more she could do about any of this tonight. She'd just have to wait until the morning.

That left just one thing to do. Scrunching down until her head rested on the pillow, Phoebe clicked off her bedside light, then pulled the covers over her head after all.

Chapter

5

"You don't think she suspected anything, do you?" Piper asked. She left her position at the bottom of the stairs, where she'd crept to make sure Phoebe had really gone to bed. Now she moved back into the living room, her fuzzy slippers making little scuffing sounds against the hardwood floor.

Paige rolled her eyes. "Why should she?" she inquired, her tone sarcastic. "Don't we act like that all the time?"

Piper flopped back down on the couch, an action that threatened to send popcorn flying into Paige's lap. "Next time, just listen to your big sister," Piper admonished. "I wanted to put the brochures away, but no—you had to keep poring over them. I had to do something to keep Phoebe away."

"Speaking of brochures," Paige said. She eyed

the bowl doubtfully. "I'm thinking we'd better rescue them before they get even more saturated with secret-recipe goop than they already are."

"Go for it," Piper nodded.

"I was afraid you'd say that," Paige remarked. Grimacing, she plunged her hand into the depths of the popcorn bowl. A moment later, she pulled it back out, clutching a handful of glossy brochures and displacing a large amount of the popcorn.

"Paige, you're making a mess," Piper complained. "Make that a bigger mess. At least take the bowl off of the couch."

Paige ignored her. "Eeeww," she exclaimed as she held the brochures at arm's length. They were covered in grease spots. "Gross. There's no way we can use those now! I don't even want to touch them. They've got gunk all over them."

This time, it was Piper who rolled her eyes. She began retrieving the scattered popcorn and tossing it into the bowl. She didn't know what was more upsetting: the food all over the living room, or wasting her secret recipe on uneaten treats.

"You've been ingesting that *gunk* all night, you know."

"On popcorn, it looks good," Paige said as she got to her feet and started toward the kitchen. "On brochures, I just don't think so. These guys are definitely trash-compactor material."

"Since when do we have a trash compactor?" Piper asked as she finished her cleanup and trailed Paige to the kitchen carrying the popcorn bowl.

"Since right now."

Before Piper realized what her youngest sister intended, Paige turned on the fawcet, drenched the brochures, then scrunched them into soggy little balls. Finally, she tossed them into the garbage can beneath the sink. "All compacted," she proclaimed proudly.

"How are you at cat food cans?" Piper inquired.

"Very funny," Paige said. She dried her hands, then leaned against the counter.

"I hate to point out the obvious," Piper began. Paige snorted. Piper ignored her. "But how are we going to conduct our research now that you've done your amazing trash-compacting number on all those brochures we went to such great lengths to collect?"

"We could do some on-site scouting," Paige suggested, her tone hopeful.

"Now, Paige, you know we discussed that," Piper said, her tone severe. "That's totally impractical."

"Okay, okay, I guess you're right," Paige pouted. Then she grinned. "Though I do think it would be fun."

"I'm sure it would be," Piper said. "But it's out of the question, and you know it. We can handle demons. We'll figure this out somehow."

"I can solve it for you in two words," Paige said, her tone smug. *"Web site."*

"You are sure the witch suspects nothing?"

In the exclusive building with the panoramic water view, the man sat with his back to the window, staring at the center of his living room carpet. Every single light in the room was on.

He knew that was the way his late-night visitor liked it.

Contrast. That was the key. The display of opposites. The thing that visited him was a tall, dark column, shaped roughly like a man. Slowly, inexorably, it was swallowing up the light with which it was surrounded. If the visitor could have worked its will, it would have devoured every single light in the universe. Even the light of unborn stars. It would have made the universe over, in *its* image this time.

As a matter of fact, he was working on it.

This was the power that the man served. The power to which he was forever bound. The one that had given him the ability to transform himself from a mere mortal into an instrument of revenge, the craving for which could never be satisfied. The power that had given him the ability to live forever, as long as he fulfilled the terms of their agreement.

This was the Power of Darkness.

Nick Gerrard took a sip from the glass of Cabernet resting on the ebony table at his elbow before he answered. The red wine was the only touch of color in the whole apartment. Everything else was black or white. Light, or its opposite.

"I hope you're not suggesting that I'm losing my touch," he remarked.

The Power of Darkness laughed. Even after all these years, it was an unsettling, uncomfortable sound, Nick thought. It reminded him of fingernails against a windowpane on a pitch-black night.

"No, no," his master said. "Of course not. But the witch might be more . . . perceptive, given who, and what, she is."

"She might be," Nick admitted, setting the glass down on the table with a sharp *click*. "But she's not. She didn't suspect a thing. Nor, for that matter, did Belthazor."

"Tut tut," Nick's visitor chided. The correction was mild, even old-fashioned, but Nick could hear the edge of rage in the dark voice. "He's not Belthazor anymore. Not after what that witch and her sisters did to him. After what he let them do."

Nick inclined his head, acknowledging the correction. It was nothing less than the truth, after all.

"The *man*, Cole Turner, suspected nothing. He was too busy with his own jealousy to pay attention to me."

As I thought. As I planned. There was a pause during which the lights in the apartment grew noticeably dimmer. *I thought that news would please you*, Nick thought.

"So," the Power of Darkness breathed at last. "You were right. His feelings for the witch will betray him in the end, just as he betrayed us."

"That's the plan," said Nick Gerrard. He took a second sip of wine.

"I *know* what the plan is," snapped the Power of Darkness. "I approved it, if you recall. But I also know how easy it is for plans to fail. All the others have, so far."

Nick set his glass of wine down, carefully. He would do well to choose his next words with the same care, he thought. He knew his master valued him. At the moment. But failure had a definite way of causing one's value to plummet precipitously. A thing the others who had failed to bring down the man who had once been Belthazor had discovered. To their ultimate cost. "May I speak plainly?" he asked, deciding on the direct approach.

"Please do," the Power of Darkness said, its tone genial now. "It's so hard to find anyone willing to tell me the truth. I can't imagine why."

"The plans you employed before lacked subtlety. They lacked finesse," said Nick Gerrard. "Belthazor, Cole, is strong. He's prepared for a direct approach. That much is obvious. That's why my plan employs an *indirect* one."

"The witch," the Power of Darkness said.

Nick nodded. "Certainly the witch," he
agreed. "But that's not all. The beauty of my
plan is that it turns Cole's own feelings, his own
choices, against him. He wanted to be human.
With that, comes human frailties. Those are the
things that will bring him down."

"So you say."

"I don't just *say*," Nick said, leaning forward
in his chair. His voice grew rough. "I *know*. I'm
an expert on how a mortal man feels when he's
betrayed. Surely you haven't forgotten that. It's
how I came to be in your service, after all."

"I haven't forgotten," said the Power of
Darkness.

Nick leaned back, struggling for control. *Nor
have I*, he thought. *Nor have I.* He would never
forget the sequence of events that had brought
him to be what he was today. Not if he really did
live forever. But it was rare for him to let the
remembering break the lock he kept on his self-
control.

"Then believe me when I say this: If Cole
Turner is half the man I think he is, he'll want
revenge, just as I did. That means I know how
far he'll be prepared to go."

The lights in the apartment dimmed once
more.

"We shall see," the Power of Darkness said
after a moment. "But you please me, as always.
Bring me the betrayer, and I will be even more
pleased. I might even be pleased enough to

give you the honor of destroying him."

"He'll destroy himself. That's what my plan is all about," Nick promised as an image of Cole Turner, the man who had once been so much more, flashed across his mind.

What kind of individual gave up the kind of power being a demon could provide? Who in their right mind would make the choice that Cole had made—the exchange that he had made?

The power of fear for the power of love.

Only a fool, thought Nick. A fool who needed to be taught a lesson. And he was just the one to do it. He grinned. "But I would appreciate a front-row seat," he said.

"Count on it," the Power of Darkness said.

And he plunged the apartment into total darkness.

Hours later, just before dawn, Nick Gerrard awoke. His heart pounding out the sharp, irregular rhythm that could only mean one thing: fear.

It's always the same, he thought.

He could assume any human form, any face he wanted. But there was one thing he could not change, could not control. Since he'd entered the service of the Power of Darkness, he hadn't been able to sleep through the night.

Not once.

Always, in the moments right before the dark gave way to light, the breathless moments when the earth itself seemed to hold its breath, wondering whether it could pull off the transition from night to day, Nick awoke. And when he did, he always did the same thing, painful though it was.

Throwing his legs over the side of the bed, Nick got up. On bare feet, he padded into the bathroom and switched on the light. *I preferred the days of candlelight,* he thought. Candlelight was kinder, less revealing. Not that it had helped. The harsh white glare of the powerful lightbulbs illuminating his face, Nick stared at himself in the mirror. Daring himself to meet his own eyes.

Then, he dared himself to keep on meeting them as the face in the mirror began to change.

Slowly, inexorably, its edges began to blur, his features, all except the eyes, subtly folding in on themselves until they vanished, and nothing of the man calling himself Nick Gerrard remained. He was a tabula rasa. A blank slate. A pair of eyes staring out of empty flesh.

So far, so good, he thought. *Two down, one to go.*

He'd been unsettled by this initial transition at first. Unprepared. The fact that he'd be forced to repeat this little ritual each and every night was a thing the Power of Darkness had conveniently left out ahead of time. But as unsettling as the first transition was, Nick knew the worst was yet to come.

He kept his eyes on the mirror as, once again, his face began to change.

Now the skin began to ridge and pucker. The surface of Nick's face, so smooth and plain just a moment before, became covered in thick red welts. The mouth curled up in an impossible grin. The eyelids turned black and drooped down. And still the transition continued until the face of the man in the mirror proclaimed he was a man no longer, but something simply impossible. Unspeakably horrible. Some freak of form for which not even nature had a name.

I can do this. I will *do it*, Nick thought. And willed himself to keep on looking.

But, at the very last second, his will faltered. His eyes shifted away, and he looked down, staring at the counter, where one fist was clenched so tightly, the knuckles writhed white.

He'd failed. Again. Just as he'd done every single morning since he'd made his devil's bargain. The powers that bargain had given him were almost limitless. But there was still one action he'd never been able to perform.

He'd never been able to look himself in the face. His true face. The one that had driven him to make his bargain in the first place.

Not once in over two hundred years had Nick Gerrard been able to bear the sight of what he truly was.

He turned and left the room, the lights that illuminated the scene of his failure bright and piercing as a scream behind him.

Chapter
6

When Phoebe awoke the next morning, a clear, white light shone down into her sleepy eyes. She closed them quickly, burrowing back down beneath the covers. Outside her window, she could have sworn she heard birds twittering and chirping.

What on earth was going on?

She rolled over, away from the window, cautiously reopened one eye, and found herself nose to nose with a single long-stemmed red rose. It literally glowed in the morning light.

Light, that was it, Phoebe thought.

Mornings in the Bay Area were almost always misty. It literally came with the territory, as San Francisco was right on the water. But this morning, the sun was out. Streaming in through Phoebe's bedroom window as strong and thick as honey.

No wonder the birds are singing, she thought.

A morning like this made her want to sing too, and a morning person was a thing she most definitely was not.

She scooted a little closer to the rose. Gave it an appreciative sniff. Beneath it was an envelope with Cole's bold handwriting scrawled across the front. Phoebe scooched her head around until she could read the words he'd written.

PHOEBE, GIRL OF MY DREAMS, the envelope said.

Phoebe felt a rush of love for him swarm through her. Inside the envelope was Cole's apology, she was sure of it. Naturally, she would have preferred for him to deliver it in person. But he'd probably had to be at the office at the crack of dawn, continuing to troubleshoot the problem that had caused him to miss their date the night before.

Instead of criticizing his choice, she'd give him points for letting her sleep, Phoebe decided. Cole knew she didn't function well first thing in the morning.

Besides, some sort of apology was definitely better than nothing.

Phoebe sat up, tucking the covers around her waist. A delicious smell was wafting up the stairs. Phoebe's guess was Piper's carrot muffins, which just happened to be her favorites, though she'd be the first to confess it was hard to find a breakfast pastry that she *didn't* like.

I'll read Cole's apology first, she decided. Then

she'd head downstairs and tackle her sisters.

The sun was shining. It was a brand-new day.

A day on which Phoebe Halliwell was going to do her darndest to make things go right.

Twenty minutes later she was showered and heading downstairs, still chuckling over Cole's "apology."

I'm sorry I lost my temper last night, Cole's note had said. *I'll try to do better next time. See you tonight. Have a nice day.*

As apologies went, it did lack a certain finesse, Phoebe acknowledged as she headed toward the good aromas coming from the kitchen, her red rose held lightly but firmly in one hand. Particularly that part about *next time.* Still, she knew what Cole meant, and he *had* made an effort.

She'd find the perfect vase, then take the rose back upstairs and place it near her side of the bed. Or maybe she'd leave it smack dab in the middle of the kitchen table, where her sisters couldn't help but notice. That ought to help relieve whatever weird feelings they were having about Phoebe and Cole's upcoming nuptials.

Okay, so Cole's apology hadn't been perfect, Phoebe thought as she rummaged for Gram's crystal bud vase in the dining room sideboard. But in the light of such a glorious morning, it was easy for her to cut him a little more slack than she had last night, in the cold and the fog.

Cole had tried. That was the important part. He'd been wrong, and he'd acknowledged it. Not much about his former existence would have prepared him for the fine art of apology-making. Being a demon *did* tend to mean never having to say you were sorry.

Besides, Phoebe thought as she tucked the vase under one arm and used her hip to push open the kitchen door, apologizing was like any other skill. It could be improved with practice. She had a feeling Cole was going to get a lot. Like, say, for instance, an entire married lifetime's worth. "Morning," she sang out as she sailed into the room.

Huddled together in front of the computer that sat in the corner where Piper often did paperwork for P3, Paige and Piper jumped about a mile.

"Phoebe!" Piper said as she whipped around and stepped in front of Paige, effectively block-ing the computer screen with her body. Behind Piper, Phoebe could hear Paige typing frantically on the keyboard. "Hey, you're up!"

Oh no, Phoebe thought. *Here we go again.* She pulled in a deep breath. *That's all right*, she told her-self. *I can handle this.* Today, she was determined not to let any sisterly weirdness bother her. "Of course I'm up," she said as she put her rose in water. A basket of Piper's carrot muffins was already sitting in the center of the table, so Phoebe placed the vase on the kitchen windowsill instead.

"It's morning. The sun's even out, in case you haven't noticed."

"The sun, yeah, great," Piper said. She didn't actually wring her hands, but Phoebe was pretty sure she wanted to. She moved to the cabinet, removed her favorite mug, then headed for the coffeepot, noticing the way Piper shifted position with every move she made, continuing to shield Paige from view. It was pretty obvious. The only way Phoebe could have failed to notice would have been if she'd been, say, blind.

Finally, coffee in hand, Phoebe leaned against the counter and took a fortifying sip. *Decisive action. That's what's in order,* she decided. Maybe if she rattled a few cages, she could find out what was going on around here.

She set her coffee cup down on the counter with a *click* and made a sudden lunge.

"What are you doing?" Piper squeaked.

"Muffin," Phoebe said. She flipped back the napkin covering the basket and held one aloft in triumph.

"What?" Piper said blankly, as if Phoebe had suddenly started speaking a foreign language.

"Muffin," Phoebe said again. With a flourish, she set the muffin down on one of the plates Piper had set out beside the basket. "You know—that thing you sometimes make in the morning that goes really great with coffee? I thought I'd have one. Unless you're planning to save them all for Leo, or something."

"Leo, of course not," Piper said. As if on cue, a white, sparkly light began to materialize right beside her.

"Leo, of course not what?" her husband asked as he fully orbed into view.

Almost before he'd finished sparkling, Piper hurled herself into his arms. "Boy, am I glad to see you!" she cried.

"Me too," Leo said, though his expression was about equal parts confusion and delight, Phoebe was quick to note. A thing that definitely perked her spirits up. Apparently, she wasn't the only one who thought Piper was behaving oddly. Cheered by Leo's confusion, Phoebe decided to treat herself. While Piper was busy greeting her husband, Phoebe snuck a second muffin onto her plate.

Whatever was up with Piper and Paige, Piper hadn't yet shared it with her husband. That meant she still had doubts about her doubts. Or something. Piper always discussed the really serious stuff with Leo. It was the way their relationship worked—one of the things Phoebe admired most about it.

"Wow, what are we having, a reunion or something?" Paige suddenly spoke up. She turned away from the computer, collapsing the window of whatever she'd been working on.

Not much chance to find out what they didn't want me to see now, Phoebe thought.

"Oh man, is that the time?" Paige went on as

her eyes focused on the kitchen clock. "I'm gonna be late. Gotta run. See you tonight, Phoebe. You'll remember to pick up my dry cleaning, right?"

Without waiting for an answer, Paige dashed around Phoebe, snatching one of the muffins from Phoebe's plate as she went, then scooted out the door.

Phoebe deliberately replaced the muffin that Paige had stolen. "I'm going back upstairs," she announced. "Yes, that is my rose on the windowsill. Yes, it *is* absolutely perfect. In case anybody's interested, it's a gift from Cole, the man I love and am going to marry. Thank you very much. That is all." She spun on one heel and marched toward the door, plate held high.

Leo's plaintive voice reached her just as she started up the stairs: "How come I'm the only one around here who never seems to know what's going on?"

Several hours later, Phoebe was piloting the SUV through the always-crowded San Francisco streets, determined to get every single errand on her list done before she had to return the vehicle to Piper. Paige might be the world's most tenacious social worker, and Piper a domestic goddess, but neither of them could hold a candle to Phoebe when it came to errand-running.

As if determined to prove it, Phoebe maneuvered the SUV around a tow truck and pounced upon a parking spot about half a block up. *Gotcha!*

she thought. This was definitely her lucky errand day. Finding a parking spot on the street in San Francisco just didn't happen all that often.

Which probably explained the tow truck, Phoebe realized suddenly.

She clambered out of the SUV, set the alarm, and retraced her steps, heading for the shop that was her destination, one that specialized in what Phoebe privately referred to as high-tech guy toys. It wasn't precisely on her list of household errands, but she'd promised herself that if there was a parking place anywhere within a two-block radius, she'd take it as a sign she should whip in and see about a gift for Cole. A little positive apology reinforcement never hurt anyone.

Ouch! Phoebe thought as she drew even with the tow truck.

With a squeal of metal against metal, the tow-truck operator was attaching big, mean-looking hooks to the undercarriage of a snazzy little red sports car. It was parked right in front of the high-tech gadget shop. Apparently, the guy who drove the sports car lacked her excellent parking karma, Phoebe thought. The car was parked in a tow-away zone. One that wasn't all that clearly marked. The sign proclaiming NO PARKING was hidden behind the enormous limb of a nearby tree.

Not that the tow-truck guy was going to let a little thing like that stop him.

The driver of the sports car was probably in the

same shop she was heading for, Phoebe realized
suddenly. With luck, he'd notice what was going
on before it was too late. Or maybe she should go
in and call out a general warning. Suddenly uncertain, Phoebe hesitated on the sidewalk.

As she watched, the tow-truck driver hitched
up his pants and stomped to the cab of the truck.
He opened the driver's door, leaned down, and
threw a lever. The engine powering the winch
gave a full-throated roar. Then, the front of the
sports car began to rise into the air as it was drawn
inexorably toward the back end of the tow truck.

"Hey!" a voice suddenly called out. "Hey,
wait a minute. Stop! That's my car!"

A figure hurtled out of the shop behind Phoebe,
almost mowing her down in his haste to reach the
curb. Hands caught and steadied her automatically, then released. But the agitated driver never
took his eyes from his sporty red coupe. "What do
you think you're doing?" he cried.

"What does it look like I'm doing, buddy?"
the tow-truck driver barked. He very definitely
had a smirk on his face. *This encounter is probably
making his entire week,* Phoebe thought. He got to
tow the sports car and taunt the driver, all at the
same time.

"But that's my car," the guy protested.

The tow-truck driver waited until the sports
car had reached its destination, front nose dan-
gling in the air from the tow bar. Then he switched
off the winch.

"That oughta make it easy for you to claim then, shouldn't it?" he asked. He reached into the pocket of his coveralls and pulled out a grease-smeared white card. "There's the address of the impound. I'd shake a leg, if I were you. Guys down there are just gonna love seein' this baby come onto the lot."

"But you can't just *take* it," the driver protested. "I haven't done anything wrong!"

"Think again," the tow-truck driver said. He gave a jerk with his thumb. As if he'd signaled to her, Phoebe pulled aside the tree branch, revealing the NO PARKING sign standing like a sentry just behind it.

"Oh," the driver of the sports car said, his expression stricken. "Oh, no."

"Guess this just isn't your day, pal," the tow-truck driver said cheerfully. He climbed into the cab and slammed the door. A moment later he revved the engine and pulled out into traffic, the red sports car waving like a flag behind the tow truck.

The driver of the sports car put a hand across his eyes. "I don't think I can bear to watch," he said.

"Can't say as I blame you," Phoebe remarked. She let the branch go and it swished back into place, covering up the NO PARKING sign once more. She fought a brief inner battle with selfishness, then gave up. He was so distracted, she could probably just continue on her way. Go on into the store. But if she did that, she wouldn't be able to repay the really big favor that she owed him. "Want a ride to the impound lot?" she offered.

"Oh, I couldn't let you do that!" the guy said, dropping his hand down from in front of his eyes. "I mean, we're total strangers, and I . . ." His voice slowed, then came to a complete stop. "Phoebe?" he said. "Phoebe Halliwell?"

"Hey, Nick," Phoebe said. And she looked into the bright green eyes of Nick Gerrard.

"You're sure you want to do this?" Nick asked, several moments later. They'd gone back into the store to retrieve his purchase. When Nick had learned why Phoebe was in the neighborhood, he'd insisted she take the time to complete her errand and pick out a gift for Cole. Phoebe'd made her selection as swiftly as she could. The two were now standing on the sidewalk beside the Halliwell SUV. "You don't have to, you know," Nick went on.

"I do know that, Nick," Phoebe said, not quite certain whether she wanted to laugh or scream. "You've only told me about half a million times."

"I'm repeating myself, aren't I?" Nick Gerrard asked. "I just don't want you to feel you have to go to any trouble, Phoebe. I mean, I don't want you to feel obligated or anything."

"And I appreciate that," Phoebe said. "I really do." She punched the button on her key ring, which unlocked the passenger's door.

When Nick stood still, hesitating on the sidewalk, Phoebe reached past him and opened the door. "If you make me say I want to do this one more time, I'm going to change my mind," she warned.

"Oh, don't do that," Nick exclaimed.

Phoebe couldn't help but smile. Reverse psychology. It worked on the male of the species every single time. "Look, Nick," she said. "For the very last time. I do *not* feel obligated. I actually *want* to drive you clear across town to the impound lot. Now will you please get in the car?"

Nick got in. "You do so," he said as Phoebe climbed in beside him.

"Do not," Phoebe said automatically as she strapped on her seat belt. There was a beat of silence. Then she laughed. "I do so what?"

"Feel obligated," Nick said as he fastened his own seat belt.

Phoebe sighed. Plainly, he was not going to be satisfied until they'd gotten over this. "Of course I do," she finally acknowledged. "Things got a little . . . uncomfortable . . . last night. But they could have been a whole lot worse. I have you to thank for the fact that they didn't. As far as I'm concerned, that means I owe you one."

"But," said Nick. Phoebe raised a hand and he fell silent.

"I know we never expected to meet again," Phoebe went on. "But since we have, I'd like to return the favor. I genuinely appreciated the way you kept your head last night."

"But it's so far," Nick protested.

"I don't care if it's on the moon," Phoebe answered promptly. "I'd like to say thank you. That means I'll take you wherever you need to go."

Nick smiled. "Say that again," he prompted.

Phoebe frowned. The shock of seeing his car towed must have been greater than she'd realized. Nick wasn't making much sense all of a sudden. "Say what?"

"That thing about where you'll take me," Nick said.

"Oh, that," Phoebe said as she decided to humor him. "I believe I said, 'I'll take you wherever you need to go.'"

"I can't tell you what it means to me to hear you say that, *witch*," Nick said.

There was a blinding flash of light, and Phoebe remembered nothing more.

Chapter

7

"What do you mean Phoebe's not home yet?" asked Cole. Cell phone pressed to one ear, he hurried down the hall toward the elevator that would take him to the parking garage. He wanted to run, but he couldn't. The hallway was crowded with office workers heading home. That's where Cole had been going, too, when Piper's call had come in.

Home. That place where Phoebe should be, but wasn't.

"Today's what?" Desperately, Cole cast his mind over what he knew about the schedule Phoebe and her sisters had worked out, trying to ignore the way his heart had begun to pound in hard, fast strokes. If anything had happened to Phoebe, he'd . . .

"Thursday. Is it Thursday? That's errand day, right?"

"Right," Piper's voice confirmed. "She took the SUV as usual this morning. She's always back by early afternoon because she knows I need it to get to P3, but she didn't show up. I didn't think much about it at first. I mean, running late happens. I took a cab to P3, and when I got there, I had to put out a couple of fires. I didn't even think about it again till I got back home and still no Phoebe."

"Did you try her cell?" Cole interrupted. He knew he was being abrupt, but he couldn't help it. Piper almost never rambled, but she was doing so now. Her manner as much as her words were telling him just how concerned about Phoebe she was.

Impatiently, Cole jabbed at the elevator button. *Come on*, he thought. *Come on.* Why, just when time was of the essence, did everything seem to be moving in slow motion?

"I just did," said Piper.

"And?"

"Nothing."

"What do you mean nothing?" Cole asked as the elevator *pinged* and the doors slid open. He joined the mass of bodies surging forward, not even noticing when he ended up pressed against the back of the elevator. What Piper was saying just didn't make sense. You didn't call a cell phone and get nothing. You got a request to leave a voice mail. An out-of-service-area message. Something.

"I mean *nothing*," Piper said, the tone of her voice rising up a notch. "Just dead air. That's when I started to worry something might be wrong. I called Paige, but she hadn't heard from Phoebe either. So then I called you and—just a minute. I think somebody's coming."

The elevator began its descent. Cole watched the floor numbers count down. Slowly.

"It isn't her," Piper's voice sounded breathlessly in his ear. "It's just Paige. I'm sorry. I think you should come home, Cole. I mean, I don't *know* that anything's wrong, but . . ." Piper's voice faltered. "Something about this just doesn't feel right, and I . . ."

"I'm on my way," Cole promised. "Just hang tight. Where's Leo?"

Without warning, Cole could hear a disturbance in the background on the cell phone. Paige's voice called out, then cut off.

"Piper!" Cole shouted, heedless of the crowded elevator around him. "Piper, what's happening? What's going on?"

There was a beat of silence, then Piper's voice sounded in his ear. She spoke two words before the connection went dead: *"Hurry, Cole."*

Cole had no idea how many potential speeding violations he racked up getting to Halliwell Manor. If he'd bothered to think about it, he'd have to figure it would be somewhere in the vicinity of "lots." He wasn't thinking about his driving, though. There was only one thing on his mind as he sent his car hurtling through the city toward the place he now called home.

Something was terribly wrong.

Something that had to do with Phoebe. Just the thought made Cole's all-too-human heart stutter and threaten to do the thing his car hadn't managed once on his way across town: come to a complete and total stop.

If something happened to Phoebe, would his mortal life even be worth living?

I won't think about it, Cole vowed as he rounded the final corner. Instead, he'd focus on the here and now. Identify the problem. Find the solution.

Find Phoebe.

With a shriek of brakes, Cole pulled up in front of Halliwell Manor, barely stopping to turn off the ignition before he leaped out of the car. He took the front walkway at a dead run. Adrenaline pumping through his system, he sent the front door crashing back and somersaulted through it, coming up into a battle crouch.

Just because he wasn't a demon anymore didn't mean he'd forgotten how to put up one hell of a fight.

But nothing rushed at him as soon as he entered. No body-searing energy bolts came carooming around the nearest corner. Cautiously, Cole straightened, the eerie silence of the house pulling at his already-stretched nerves. "Piper? Paige?" he called out.

"In here," Piper's voice replied after a moment, the tone strange and high. He heard her clear her throat, then try again. "We're in the dining room, Cole. I think it would be a good idea if you came in here too. Just do me a favor, will you?"

"What?" Cole said. Every sense in his body on red-alert, he began to move toward the dining room as silently as he could, keeping his back against the wall.

"No sudden moves, huh? Just come in nice and slow. He says it will be better for us all that way."

Cole stopped moving. "Who says?" he called. He was almost there, he thought. Just a few more steps and he'd be able to . . .

"I did," said a new voice. One that somehow managed to sound low and gravelly, yet snake-like, all at the same time. Something definitely not human, Cole decided. Not that that came as a really big surprise.

"Whatever mortal heroics you're planning, you can just forget about them," the unknown demon's voice went on. "Just do as the lady says. No sudden moves. Come in nice and slow. I'm not looking for a fight. All I want is the chance to deliver a message. You really want to hear what I have to say."

"I doubt it," said Cole.

The demon laughed. It was an ugly sound. "Trust me," he said. "You do not want to screw this up. If you do, you'll never see your witch again."

Phoebe, Cole thought, panicking.

Every instinct Cole had was urging him to hurry, yet he forced himself to hesitate, to consider his options. Almost more than anything in the world, he wanted to do the opposite of what the unknown demon said. Strike hard and fast, first. Ask questions second.

But more than he wanted to give in to the impulse to strike, he wanted to know that Phoebe was safe. It seemed pretty obvious now that she'd been taken. He didn't know by whom. Or what. Regardless, the priority had to be gathering the information that would help get Phoebe back. Much as Cole hated to admit it, listening to the demon messenger was his best way of accomplishing that.

So, he'd let demon-boy have his say, *then* he'd take him apart, Cole decided. That way, he could satisfy both the practical needs of the situation, and the need to pound on something that was raging through his blood.

Satisfied with the course of action he'd chosen, Cole sucked in a breath and stepped into the open.

He saw Piper and Paige seated back to back in two dining room chairs, their arms bound tightly together. Hardly the world's most original choice, but it did provide the added benefit of putting Piper's time-freezing abilities out of commission. She had to be able to move her hands to activate those. Paige probably hadn't trusted her orbing powers to remove the two of them to safety. Besides, no matter where they went, they'd still be tied up.

"You okay?" Cole asked, his eyes on Piper. She nodded.

Cole turned his attention to the only other being in the room. Standing at the far end of the table was a short demon with a scaly green face. He was dressed in a parody of the business attire Cole himself wore. White button-down shirt, neatly pressed pants. A jacket and tie. He was polishing off what appeared to be the remains of a basket of Piper's carrot muffins.

"You should try one of these. They're not half bad," he said, giving Cole a sharp-fanged smile.

"You wanted me, I'm here," Cole replied. "Suppose we skip the preliminary demon chat and go right to the part where you tell me why *you're* here."

The demon ran a forked tongue across his lips. "Being a mortal hasn't improved your temper, I see."

Cole took a menacing step forward.

"All right. All right," the demon said, taking a quick step back before he could stop himself. "Geez, what a grouch. Look around you. Notice anything missing? Or maybe I should say, any*one*."

"Of course I do," Cole snapped. "I'm human, not stupid. Somebody's snatched Phoebe, haven't they? Where is she, and what do they want?"

"Ah, but there's the beauty of it," the demon said, its tongue snaking out for the second time.

He's enjoying this, Cole thought. *A lot. Too much.*

"There was absolutely no snatching involved. She went of her own free will," the demon continued. He waved one arm, scattering muffin crumbs. "Behold!"

As if the wall of the dining room had suddenly become a movie screen, Cole, Paige, and Piper watched the scene unfold.

They saw Phoebe, standing on the sidewalk in front of what Cole recognized as his favorite high-tech gadget shop. She appeared to be watching in concern as a red sports car was being towed. Standing nearby was what had to be the car's owner, if his reaction to the tow was anything to go by.

What does this have to do with anything? Cole thought. He was just opening his mouth to frame the question, when he saw Phoebe's lips move. In response, the guy turned around.

Cole felt the breath leave his body as if he'd taken a fist straight to the gut. He knew this guy. He'd have known him anywhere. It was Phoebe's dinner companion from the night before.

"You're beginning to get the picture, I see," the demon commented, his beady little eyes intent on Cole's face. "You're quick, even if you are a grouch. You recognize him, then?"

Cole nodded, not certain he could trust his voice. First dinner, then a meeting the next day. Had Phoebe's outrage been faked? Had she betrayed him after all?

"Wait a minute—you're saying this guy's connected with the underworld?" Paige suddenly spoke up. "No way. He looks more like the kid on those *Andy Griffith Show* reruns."

"Looks can be deceiving," the scaly-green-very-obviously-a-demon said. "In *his* case. . . ." With a jerk of his head, he indicated the guy with Phoebe. In the scene being played back on the wall, the two were in earnest conversation now.

"In his case, more than most. He can have one face when he wakes up in the morning, another in the afternoon, an entirely different one at night. The possibilities are literally endless. And no two faces are ever alike. Nobody has ever seen the real one. Not even him, or so the whispers go."

"Why not?" Paige asked. "Not that I'm all that sure I really want to know."

"Simple," the demon answered. "Because his face is so terrifying, not even he can bear to look upon it."

Cole felt the blood drain from his pounding

head. There was only one thing he knew that matched that description. A thing that had once been human but was something entirely different. None of it good. And in way too close proximity to the woman he loved.

His eyes glued to the wall, Cole watched as Phoebe urged one of the most dangerous beings in the underworld into the passenger seat of the Halliwell SUV.

"Tauschung."

Chapter

8

"Gezundheit," Paige said automatically.

The demon laughed in delight. "I'm beginning to see why you like it around here," he said to Cole. "These witches are just a laugh-riot."

Cole felt his temper snap like a guitar string pulled too tight. He covered the distance between himself and the demon in three quick strides. Seizing the demon by the neck, he lifted him straight up into the air.

"Is he supposed to be able to do that?" Paige asked anxiously. "I mean, now that he's a mere mortal and all?"

"I guess *mere* is a subjective term," Piper answered, twisting around to try to see what was going on.

Their exchange was silenced by the sound of Cole's hard and angry voice. "Do you see me laughing?" he asked the demon.

The demon made a choking sound.

"I didn't think so," Cole said. "Where has he taken her? Show me the rest of it. Do it *now*."

Feet kicking in the air, the demon waved his hands, and the scene on the wall began to move at a more rapid pace. Phoebe was climbing into the car now. The scaly green demon made a second gesture. Phoebe's voice filled the dining room: "I'll take you wherever you need to go."

"I was hoping you'd say that," said the guy beside her. There was a blinding flash of light. Phoebe and her companion vanished. The images on the wall winked out.

"Where is she?" Cole demanded. Rage and fear coursed through his system in hot, thick waves. He shook the demon like a rag doll. Through the roaring in his ears, he could hear Piper's voice, speaking urgently: "Cole, *Cole!* Put him down! He can't answer with your hand wrapped around his throat."

"She's right," a new voice said. Cole felt a hand descend upon his shoulder. Before he could snarl a *back-off* warning, he realized who it was.

"He's not the thing we need to fight. He's just the messenger," Leo said. "Come on, Cole, put him down. Let him tell us what he knows. That's the important thing."

He's right, Cole thought. *I have got to get myself back under control.* If he didn't, Phoebe might be lost forever.

Slowly, Cole lowered the demon to the floor.

Then, with Leo beside him, he retreated back across the room until he'd once more put the dining table between himself and the demon. He wasn't quite sure he'd be able to trust himself, otherwise.

"You've got about two more seconds to tell us what you know."

"She's in the underworld, where do you think?" the demon snarled. "She went there of her own free will. You heard that for yourself. You ask me, your witch girlfriend's pulled a fast one on you, O, he-who-used-to-be-Belthazor. Got you to give up your powers, then traded you in for a newer, better model. *Tauschung*'s pretty far up there on the old demon hierarchy. Right under the Power of Darkness."

Tell me something I don't know, Cole thought. Like, how to get her back. He tried to force the question out, but his throat seemed frozen.

"How do we get her back?" Leo asked, echoing Cole's thoughts.

The demon sneered. "Isn't it obvious? Mortal-boy here has to go down and rescue her—assuming he actually can, of course. If he can find her and claim her, he can bring her back to this world. If not, they both stay down below. Personally, I wouldn't bet a nickel on his chances. He didn't stand much of a chance against a thing like *Tauschung*, even when he was a demon. Now?"

The demon shook its head. "But I *am* a little biased, I admit. Okay, so. Now where did I put that thing?" He began to pat his pockets, searching for something. "Oh, there it is!" he exclaimed after a moment, extracting a cylindrical object from his back pants pocket. "Ever notice how things are always in the last place you look? *Catch!*" With one sudden gesture, he flipped the thing he'd located through the air toward Cole.

Adrenaline surged through Cole's body, fight or flight, even as his discipline kicked in and his hand moved to snatch the whatever-it-was out of the air. "A kazoo," Cole said as he studied the object. "You're giving me a *kazoo*? What the hell is this for?"

"To summon your guide, of course," the demon replied. "You are at somewhat of a disadvantage now, you know. You can't just zap yourself down to the old 'hood, the way you used to. Now you have to have a guide, just like all the other mortals. Which reminds me . . ."

He dug a hand into his jacket pocket and pulled out a shiny new coin. He balanced it on his thumbnail, then flicked it into the air. It tumbled end over end as it made its way toward Cole. "Penny for the ferryman," the demon said with an evil grin. "I think that about covers it. Message delivered. Mission accomplished. Let the games begin. I'd wish you good luck, but I wouldn't mean it, so what's the point?" One hand whisking out to capture the last of Piper's carrot muffins, he disappeared in a cloud of foul-smelling green smoke.

"Boy, am I ever glad to see you," Piper said as Leo hurried to release the bonds that held the two sisters together as soon as the demon had departed.

"I got here as soon as I could. Sorry it wasn't sooner," Leo said. Piper hurled herself into his arms the moment she was free.

"Hey—I could use a hug, too, you know," Paige remarked.

Together, Piper and Leo turned, including her in the moment. Paige gave the two others a final quick squeeze, then stepped back. As if her actions had been the signal, all three turned to face Cole.

He was staring at the wall on which the demon had revealed what had happened to Phoebe, one fist clenched around the items the demon had tossed him—his tickets back into the underworld, the place he'd tried so hard to leave behind.

For a moment, no one spoke.

"So, what's the plan?" Paige asked. "How are we going to make sure you can—what is it again? Find Phoebe and claim her? What is up with that, by the way? That is so hokey. What do they think she is—a piece of lost luggage?"

Slowly, Cole turned to face the others. His

body felt stiff and awkward. As if, if he moved too fast, the rage, the fear, and pain coursing through his veins would simply explode right out of him. "What they think," he said, in a quiet voice, "is that Phoebe is the perfect instrument for revenge against me. And you know what? They're absolutely right."

Chapter

9

"Okay, wait a minute," Paige said. "Maybe I'm just having a stupid moment, but I'm not getting this at all. You're saying they snatched Phoebe and they don't even want her?"

"Oh, they want her, all right," Cole said grimly. "It's just that they want me more. They're certainly making it easy enough for me to go looking for her, wouldn't you say? That ought to tell you something. I'm the actual target. Phoebe's just a bonus."

"I agree with Cole," Piper spoke up. "That nasty little muffin-snatching messenger demon came looking for him, not for us. But we can't afford to forget that keeping Phoebe permanently in the underworld would serve one other important purpose: It would break up the power of the Charmed Ones."

There was a moment of silence.

"Well, then, we'll just have to get her back,"
Paige said, her tone vehement. "I'm still getting
used to this being a witch idea, for crying out
loud. What do those guys think I am—
Life-Altering Transitions R Us?"

At Paige's flip words, Piper smiled. It had
taken her a while to tune in to Paige's wavelength,
but by now she understood that Paige was often
the most sarcastic when she cared the very most.

"What do you know about this sneeze demon
thing that's taken Phoebe?" Piper asked as she
turned to Cole.

"Wait a minute—a *sneeze* demon?" Leo interrupted. "There's no such thing."

"She's talking about *Tauschung*," said Cole.

Leo's face turned from thoughtful to grave.
"Uh-oh."

"You can say that again," said Cole.

"I could, but I won't."

"That bad, huh?" Piper said.

"Actually, I'd have to say I think it's worse,"
Leo admitted.

"How *much* worse?" Paige inquired.

"About as bad as it gets," Cole replied. "Our
scaly green friend wasn't kidding when he said
Tauschung was practically at the top of the bad-
guy hierarchy. He reports directly to the Power
of Darkness, and he's right behind the Source."

"So what's the story on this *Tauschung*?"
Piper asked.

"To tell you the truth," Cole admitted, "I don't know the whole story, just the underworld scuttlebut. Very bad. Very powerful. Definitely a guy to stay away from. I don't know how he got that way."

Piper and Paige exchanged significant glances.

"Everybody upstairs," Piper commanded. "*Now.*"

"According to *The Book of Shadows*," Piper said a few moments later, "the being now known as *Tauschung* was once a French aristocrat named Nicolas Gerrard."

From his position just inside the attic door, Cole made a strangled sound.

"What?" Paige said. She'd been peering over Piper's shoulder at *The Book of Shadows*. Now she turned to peer at Cole.

"Nothing," Cole answered shortly. *Just something I should have picked up on, but didn't*, he thought. *Nick Gerrard*. If he'd made the connection last night, if he hadn't been so blinded by his own jealousy that he hadn't paid attention to anything else, would Phoebe be safe now?

Don't think that way, he told himself fiercely. If he gave in to that kind of thinking, despair would be the inevitable result. He'd be playing right into the bad guys' hands, a thing he'd obviously already done once. And once was more than enough. "Go on," he said aloud.

"During the French Revolution," Piper continued, "a band of marauders set fire to Gerrard's château. He almost burned to death. Only the fact that he'd taken the unaristocratic action of getting engaged to a local peasant girl allowed him to survive. Her family risked their lives to rescue him. They barely got him out in time."

"All this makes him sound like kind of a good guy," Paige commented. "How'd he end up reporting to the Power of Darkness?"

Piper turned the page and scanned *The Book of Shadows* for a moment.

"Apparently, when Gerrard's fiancée saw how badly he'd been burned, she totally freaked," she explained. "Declared she could never marry such a monster. At which point Gerrard vowed revenge. Said he'd show her, and all womankind, just what a monster was. The Power of Darkness overheard him and essentially offered him the power to do exactly that—in exchange for an eternity in his service, of course."

"Some bargain," Paige commented.

"Actually, if you want to spend eternity getting even, it's a pretty good deal," Leo said. It was the first time he'd spoken since they'd come to consult *The Book of Shadows*.

"So what exactly are his powers?" Paige asked.

"I'm not quite sure," Piper said, her eyes on *The Book of Shadows*. "'*And he took for himself the name and the power of* Tauschung,'" she read out loud. "That's all it says."

"Well, that's clear as mud," Paige commented.

"Actually," Leo put in, "it's not quite that bad. Gerrard's demon name, *Tauschung*, means 'illusion.'"

"So, he took the name and power of illusion?" Piper asked.

"That's right." Leo nodded. "*Tauschung*'s power is the ability to assume whatever form he wants, though I don't think he's ever chosen to be anything other than a human man. But he can assume whatever face he chooses. He can look like anyone."

"You mean he could look like one of you?" Paige asked. Her eyes darted between Leo and Cole as if she expected them to change shape right before her.

"He could," Cole answered, his voice grim. "But he wouldn't. Masquerading as someone else is definitely not his style. *Tauschung*'s faces are always tailor-made to fit his chosen victim. The face he assumes meets some need she has, even if she doesn't realize it herself. Then, when she's committed herself to him, he betrays her, just as he was betrayed. That's how he gets his revenge."

"'*For the master, the souls, for the minion, the bargain,*'" Piper read from *The Book of Shadows*. "Well, now I guess we know how the setup works. The Power of Darkness gets the souls of *Tauschung*'s victims, and *Tauschung* himself gets a continuation of his powers."

"Sounds right." Cole nodded.

"Well, there's the loophole, right there," Piper said, her tone growing excited. "Actually, I think it may be two loopholes. If I'm understanding correctly the bargain he made, this guy *Tauschung* isn't actually a demon. He's a souped-up mortal, backed by the Power of Darkness. What if *Tauschung* failed to deliver a soul? Wouldn't that mean he'd broken his part of the bargain? The Power of Darkness could cut him off. Terminate his powers and his life."

"In theory, I suppose you're right," Cole admitted. "*Tauschung*'s never failed to deliver yet, though."

"He's never dealt with one of the Charmed Ones before, has he?" Piper answered.

"Not one," Paige said firmly. "All. Plus reinforcements."

"You got that right," Piper said, giving her youngest sister a swift hug around the shoulders. "Now all we need is a plan of attack."

"I still don't get how that corn-fed Iowa farm-boy face fulfilled some secret need of Phoebe's," Paige interrupted, her face wrinkling in disbelief. "What is up with that, anyhow?"

"Well," Piper said consideringly, "if you think about it, a face like that could be described as the opposite of Cole's."

"Okay, I think I'm getting the way this works," Paige said slowly. "Cole turned out to have deep, dark depths, right? So *Tauschung* deliberately selected a face for Phoebe that looked as if it would have nothing to hide—"

"When, in fact," Piper picked up the explanation, "it did. Specifically, something a whole lot worse than Belthazor ever was."

"Definitely diabolical," Paige commented. "How did Phoebe even meet this guy?"

Cole took a deep breath. *Time to come clean*, he thought. And then it was past time to get down to the business of rescuing Phoebe. What Piper had called the plan of attack. "They had dinner last night."

Paige and Piper both regarded him in astonishment. *"What?"* they cried.

"Last night," Cole explained, fighting to keep his tone even, "Phoebe and I were supposed to have dinner at Chez Richard. Remember?"

"Oh yeah," Paige said softly, her eyes sliding to Piper's.

"I got held up at the office and couldn't make it," Cole went on. "Phoebe said she tried you guys, but you said you couldn't either. You wanted to stay home."

Piper closed her eyes, as if against a sudden pain. Leo moved to stand beside her. "Piper?" he prompted, his tone gentle.

"She's right," Piper answered, opening her eyes. "That's what we said."

"Well, apparently our pal *Tauschung* was at the restaurant," Cole went on. "When I finally shook loose and got over there, he and Phoebe were having dinner together, though of course I didn't recognize him at the time. I thought she was just out with some guy."

Paige winced. "Bet I can guess how that went over," she murmured.

"You'd be right," Cole said, baring his teeth in an unamused smile. "I didn't handle the situation very well."

"So, if Piper or I had gone to dinner when Phoebe asked us, none of this would have happened," Paige said.

"No, if *I'd* gone to dinner with her it wouldn't have," Cole contradicted.

"Maybe not right away," Leo put in, before the blame game could escalate. "But it would only have been a delay. *Tauschung* wouldn't have just given up and moved on.

"He targeted Phoebe for a specific reason. If the restaurant idea didn't pan out, he'd have found some other way of getting her alone. Beating yourselves up about what happened won't do any good. Assigning blame isn't going to help get Phoebe back."

"But why go for Phoebe in the first place?" Paige demanded. "If Cole's the real target, why not just go after him directly?"

"That's pretty much what they've been doing," Cole said. "And it hasn't been getting them very far. This is obviously a new tactic, designed to do one thing."

"What?"

"Bring me to them," Cole said simply. "They want me, I say they can have me. I'm going to the underworld to bring Phoebe back home."

Chapter

10

"Oh no, you don't!" Piper protested at once. "At least, not alone."

"Alone's what they want, so that's the way it's going to be," Cole came back. "I already screwed up and let them get their hands on Phoebe in the first place. I'm not going to screw the rescue up, too, Piper." Turning on his heel, he headed back down the stairs, the others following.

"But you can't just give them what they want," Piper argued as she charged after him. "You'll be playing into their hands. Walking into a trap." She turned suddenly to Paige and Leo, who were right behind her. "Can someone please jump in here before I sound even more like a bad sixties cop show?"

Cole continued his descent, his long legs eating up the stairs. He reached the ground floor and headed for the front door.

"Look, we've already established Phoebe's not the main target. I'm the one *Tauschung* and his master really want. That means the best way to spring Phoebe is to let the bad guys have me—or think that they do. If they think they hold all the cards, maybe they'll get cocky and make a mistake."

"If you follow Phoebe into the underworld, they won't have to make a mistake, because they *will* hold all the cards," Piper all but yelled. She dashed around Cole, positioning herself between him and the door.

"She does have a point," Leo said quietly.

Cole rounded on him. "And what are you suggesting as an alternative?" he asked. "That I should let you go? Do you have any idea how much everything down there would love to sink their nasty pointed teeth and claws into a Whitelighter?"

"A pretty good one," Leo said steadily. "That doesn't mean it shouldn't be considered as a potential plan."

"No way," Cole said, shaking his head. "I'm going alone, and that's final."   •

"I don't think so, Cole," Paige said. Her unusually serious tone drew all eyes to her as she moved to stand beside Leo. "Phoebe loves you. That makes you part of the family. There's no such thing as going in alone. We're all in this together, whether you like it or not. Stop thinking like a demon and think like a human."

Cole opened his mouth to snap out a reply, then closed it again. The extent of human compassion, generosity, never ceased to surprise him. For the first time since he'd learned that Phoebe was missing, Cole felt a surge of hope. "All right. Point taken," he said. "And it isn't that I don't appreciate your offer, Leo. But I can't let you go, and I think we both know why."

In silence, Cole met the other man's eyes. He and Leo didn't see eye to eye very often—figuratively or literally. Their backgrounds were simply too different. But Paige's words had made clear how much Cole and Leo now had in common: the women they loved. That meant they shared a desire and dedication to protect them, not just because they loved them, but because they were the Charmed Ones.

"Let's think about this totally rationally for a moment," Cole continued, turning to include Piper in the conversation. "My feelings for Phoebe aside."

Though the sense of time ticking away felt like a constant itch at the back of his neck, Cole now knew better than to go off half cocked. He'd done that last night with Phoebe, with disastrous results. *This is my mess. It's up to me to clean it up.*

But maybe, just maybe, Paige was right, and he didn't have to do it alone.

Cole made a gesture ushering the others

toward the living room. He waited until they'd arranged themselves around the room before he spoke. "We all agree that the one who undertakes the rescue mission faces pretty steep odds?" he asked.

"We all agree," Piper said, nodding.

"Then it seems to me that the one who actually enters the underworld needs to have certain attributes," Cole plowed on. "Particularly since they'll be about the only things he—"

"Or she," Piper murmured.

"Or she," Cole acknowledged, "has going for her. Him. Whatever. Number one: The rescuer should be as familiar with the enemy territory as possible. Number two: Much as we all might prefer not to admit it, whoever goes should be considered expendable. I possess both those attributes. Nobody else does."

There was a silence.

"You're not expendable, Cole," Piper said at last. "Phoebe loves you."

"I know that," Cole said. "But *you* know what I mean, Piper. Paige suggested I think like a human, so I am. The world can't afford to lose a Whitelighter, no matter how much Phoebe and I love each other. And it can't afford to lose the power of the Charmed Ones. That means I'm the one who has to go into the underworld, no matter what's waiting for me. Even if showing up there is exactly what the bad guys want. The picture is bigger than just Phoebe and me."

"Cole's right," Paige spoke up quietly. "It's bad enough those demon creeps have their ugly mitts on Phoebe. We can't run the risk of them taking Leo, too." Her glance slid to Piper. "Or one of us."

"So, it's decided," Cole said. "I'm going."

"Okay, so it's decided," Piper said. She threw up her hands as if she'd just given up on an argument. "You're going. But before you do, there's something else we need to figure out."

"Like what?" Cole asked.

"Like how the rest of us are going to provide you with some totally kick-ass backup."

Fifteen minutes later, they'd worked out the details.

Not that there were all that many of them.

"Okay, so we're all clear on this?" asked Cole.

Piper, Paige, and Leo nodded solemnly.

"Stage one, I go to the underworld in search of Phoebe," Cole continued.

"Stage two, I perform a special scrying spell that lets the rest of us keep an eye on you," Piper picked up where he left off. "Though I still think you ought to let me scry for Phoebe while I'm at it. Maybe that would give you a clue."

"And you'd get the information to me, how?" Cole asked. He shook his head.

"But—," Piper began.

"Piper," Leo said, the faintest edge of frustration

tinging the patience in his voice. "Cole is right, and you know it. A scrying spell that will reveal things in the underworld is both dangerous and powerful. Let Cole concentrate on locating Phoebe."

"But—," Piper began again.

Cole moved to take her by the shoulders. "Listen to me, Piper. You want me to think like a mortal? I am, and I have a mortal hunch. *Tauschung* chose his powers because he'd been betrayed. Specifically, he'd been betrayed by the woman he loved. I have a feeling that means he *wants* me to find Phoebe. No matter what his master has in store for me at the end, I'm willing to bet *Tauschung*'s got an agenda all his own. One we may be able to use to our advantage."

"Besides," Paige put in, "the scrying spell for Cole's whereabouts has to be as strong as possible. We have to know where he is. If we don't, we can't back him up."

"All right," Piper said, her tone grumpy. "*But* I still don't like it."

"Did she just get the last word in?" Cole asked Leo. In spite of the seriousness of the situation, his mouth quirked up in a half grin as he dropped his hands from Piper's shoulders.

Leo shrugged. "Always does."

"So, you get to the underworld and you find Phoebe," Paige said. "We'll know when you find her because of Piper's totally excellent scrying spell. Then, once you're reunited, I'll orb in, then orb us all back here, where we belong."

"That's the plan," Cole agreed. "Though I think we can figure it'll be a whole lot easier said than done."

"How will you get to the underworld?" Piper asked.

Cole gave a grim smile and held out the kazoo. "I'll use this to summon my guide. And I'll use *this*"—he held up the penny—"to pay him for the crossing over."

"Charon, the ferryman," Leo said.

Cole nodded.

"But I thought that was just a myth," Paige protested. "The Greeks, right?"

"Even a myth has to have its origins somewhere," Cole said. "In this case, the Greeks pretty much got it right. Though since Charon's usual passengers aren't among the living, I don't think I'll summon him from here."

"From where, then?" Paige asked.

"Where else?" Cole answered. "The nearest graveyard." He turned to Piper, yanking one of the cufflinks off from his shirt as he did so. "Here," he said, handing her the cufflink. "The link for the scrying spell will be stronger if you include something of mine. I've been wearing this all day, so the connection should be good. Not only that, they were a gift from Phoebe."

"Good," said Piper.

"Give me fifteen minutes or so to get to the graveyard and call for Charon, then fire up the scrying spell," Cole said. "I have no idea what they're going to try to throw at me down there, so whatever you see happening, try to think positive."

"We will," Piper said seriously. "Cole."

"What?" Cole asked. Almost before he got the word out, Piper threw her arms around him from one side just as Paige did so from the other. The force of the contact made Cole stagger a step. He felt Leo's steadying hand on his shoulder.

Family, Cole thought. If there was one thing the events of the day had taught him already, it was that there was no denying the bond. Unexpectedly, Cole felt a surge of energy move through him, unlike anything he'd ever felt before. *This is what I chose, what I want*, he thought. And felt the truth of it sink into his bones.

Sure, in some ways he was now weaker than when he'd been a demon. But that didn't mean he was *weak*. He was human. He wasn't alone. Even in the underworld, the others would be with him, and not just because of Piper's scrying spell. He would carry them with him, in his heart. In his hopes for the future.

A thing no demon could ever understand, because it was a thing no demon was capable of.

"Good luck," Leo said as the embrace broke up. "We'll be waiting for you."

Chapter
11

Phoebe came to with a raging headache and a sour taste in the back of her mouth. Through her closed eyelids, the light had a funny red glow.

Uh-oh, she thought. Daytime light in San Francisco could be many things. Red definitely wasn't one of them. In fact, red inevitably reminded her of . . .

Phoebe's eyes shot open, which definitely made her headache worse. She ignored it. A first quick scan of her surroundings failed to confirm her worst fears. As far as she could tell, she wasn't in close proximity to the fires of a place she seriously preferred not to name. Instead, she was in an elaborately decorated room. In front of her were several candelabrum positioned in front of opulent red curtains. It was this combination that had given off the strange red glow.

Moving gingerly, Phoebe pushed herself into a full sitting position. *What on earth?* she wondered. She was lying on what looked for all the world like a psychoanalysts's couch. Apparently, somebody was of the opinion that she needed her head examined.

"Ah, you're awake, I see," said a voice she recognized.

Phoebe whipped her head around. Sitting just behind her, in a straight-backed chair with an elaborate needlepoint seat cushion, was the last person she remembered seeing before the lights went out. "Nick," she croaked.

"Hello, Phoebe," Nick said. His tone was pleasant, maybe even self-satisfied. He rose and moved his chair, placing it in front of the curtains so Phoebe didn't have to crane her neck to see him.

"I hope you aren't experiencing too many unpleasant side effects from our little trip," he continued as he sat back down.

Make that uh-oh times two, Phoebe thought.

Nick was not behaving like a guy who was feeling he was in some sort of danger. He was behaving like a guy who figured he was in complete control. Which could pretty much mean just one thing: Whatever was going on, Nick had engineered it.

Belatedly, danger bells began to clang in the back of Phoebe's mind. *So much for the Charmed Ones' early warning system,* she thought. *Why didn't it kick in about twenty-four hours ago?*

Phoebe could feel Nick's unusual green eyes on her face. He was watching her with an intent expression that made her feel like a bug under a microscope. *He's waiting to see what I'll do next,* she thought.

Screaming for help had a certain appeal. Not that Phoebe was going to succumb. In the first place, it wouldn't do any good. In the second, it would reveal to Nick how frightened she was. Better to give him a taste of his own medicine, Phoebe decided. He wanted to look? Let him. It would give her the opportunity to do a little looking of her own.

The first thing Phoebe noticed was that Nick had changed his clothes. Gone was the pair of jeans and casual crewneck sweater he'd worn before. In their place was . . . actually Phoebe wasn't quite sure what the garments Nick was now wearing were called. Whatever they were, they made him look like he'd stepped right out of a historical painting in a museum.

Nick's pants, which Phoebe was pretty sure were made of silk, now ended at the knee. Below them were richly embroidered silk stockings. On his feet were leather shoes with polished gold buckles. An elaborately ruffled shirt flowed down his chest, the ruffles foaming like white water. A tight, form-fitting coat stretched across his broad shoulders.

Only his hair remained the same: still pulled

back and bound at the nape of his neck, though now it was held in place with a black silk ribbon.

He looks like an aristocrat, Phoebe thought.

A look that could have been ridiculous, but wasn't. In it, Nick emanated pure power, absolute confidence. It was almost as if this was how he was meant to look, Phoebe thought. How he'd looked underneath his contemporary casualness all along.

Phoebe made a split-second decision, of the "never let them see you sweat" variety. Either Nick was an everyday wacko with one heck of a costume collection, or she was in a whole lot of trouble, most likely of the supernatural kind.

"So," she said briskly as she swung her legs over the side of the psychoanalyst's couch. The action made her head swim and her stomach lurch. Phoebe fought through the sensations of discomfort. *Use it*, she thought.

It was better for her to know the truth about her physical limitations as soon as possible, so she could get to work on getting over them. A girl never knew when she was going to have to fight.

Or run.

"Do we have to wear a costume to get your car out of impound?" she inquired brightly. "I hope mine's as pretty as yours."

Nick threw back his head and laughed. "Oh, Phoebe," he said. "I am enjoying this even more than I had thought. I was focusing on the end result, you see. I had no idea that getting there would be so much fun."

"Kidnapping women is your idea of fun?" Phoebe asked, trying not to think about how much she didn't appreciate the mention of some mysterious end result.

"But I didn't kidnap you," Nick protested. "You said you'd take me wherever I needed to go. It just happened to be here, and not the impound lot. I never had any intention of going there, you know."

"I'm figuring it out, thanks," Phoebe said aloud. "Okay, I'll bite. Where am I?"

"Home," Nick Gerrard answered simply. "My home, that is. Though it's just a replica, of course. Of my family's château. It had been in our family for generations, before those *revolutionaries*"—Nick spat the word out as though it were a curse—"those pigs, burned it to the ground."

Château. That's French, Phoebe thought. So Nick's look was French Revolution, or right before. Phoebe wasn't sure what figuring that out was going to accomplish, but if there was one thing she'd learned since becoming a Charmed One, it was that every little bit of information helped.

"It's beautiful, don't you think?" Nick asked, gesturing to the room.

To Phoebe's surprise, he sounded as if he truly wanted her opinion. Once again, she looked around. The room seriously reminded her of articles in glossy lifestyle magazines. *How the Rich and Famous Live and You Don't.* Not exactly her style. She preferred things a bit more homey, herself. The living room at Halliwell Manor sounded pretty good right about now. "So, we're in France?" she asked, fishing for more information.

"Not exactly," Nick replied. "My . . . master prefers that my permanent residence be close to him."

Okay, now we're getting somewhere, Phoebe thought. She hadn't missed the slight hesitation over the word *master.* A hesitation that made a cold fear settle in the pit of her stomach. The possibility that her presence here had anything to do with the everyday world was growing more dim by the moment. Which could only mean one thing:

Nick knew that she was one of the Charmed Ones.

Phoebe decided it was time to get all the way to her feet, pleased to discover that her headache seemed to be subsiding. She wasn't up to full fighting strength yet, but it was just a matter of time. Time she fully intended to use to find out as much as possible about what was going on.

"Master, huh?" she commented. "Well, that part makes sense, at least. I mean, let's face it. You do seem more like an errand boy than the guy in charge. So, who pulls your strings, Nick? Anybody I know?"

"Nobody pulls my strings," Nick snapped, his face coloring as he scrambled up to face her. It was as much emotion as Phoebe had ever seen him show. "Nobody pulls the strings of a Gerrard."

A moment later, he gave a short laugh and settled back into his chair, stretching his legs out in front of him as if perfectly at ease. "A hit," he acknowledged. "That was clever of you. Very well done. But one hit doesn't win a battle, Phoebe. It doesn't even win the fight. Particularly since you're on your own."

Again, Phoebe felt Nick's eyes settle on her face. "Your sisters can't help you here, you know," he said.

Well, that pretty much settles things, Phoebe thought as she struggled not to let her dismay show. She was definitely here because she was a Charmed One. Not only that, she'd pretty much had her worst fears confirmed on the subject of where *here* was. There weren't too many places where her sisters would have a hard time rendering assistance.

The underworld was one.

"So why pick me?" she asked. "Why not Paige or Piper?"

"They don't have what I want. You do," Nick said simply.

Phoebe felt a chill shoot straight down her spine. She was so accustomed to being a target in her own right, she'd all but forgotten she could have another function: as bait for someone else.

"Cole," she said. "He's the one you really want. The energy-bolt-through-the-chest stuff wasn't working, was it? So you thought you'd try a sneakier approach."

"I prefer to think of it as a more human approach," said Nick Gerrard. "That's what Cole is now, isn't it? All he is. *Human*."

Phoebe could hear the sneer in Nick's voice. Desperately, she strove to push her fear for Cole to the back of her mind. Nick's behavior was telling her something, something important. She had to stay focused, to discover what it was.

"He did that for you, didn't he?" Nick went on. "Gave up his powers. Made himself weak. He's going to try to rescue you in spite of that, of course. Tell me something, Phoebe. When he fails—when he's destroyed before your very eyes—do you think you'll feel responsible?"

"No," Phoebe whispered as she momentarily lost the struggle to control her fear.

"No, you won't feel responsible—or no, you don't think he'll be destroyed?" Nick inquired. "Not that it makes any difference, of course."

Phoebe gazed into Nick's face, open and boyish, such a contrast to the face of the man she loved. "Why are you doing this?" she asked.

"And don't tell me it's your master's will. There's another reason, a more personal reason. What is it? I want to know."

"To teach him a lesson!" Nick Gerrard cried. Without warning, he sprang to his feet and began to pace around the room, his hard-soled shoes sounding like gunfire against the polished floor. "To show him the truth, before my master deprives him of his miserable life."

Definitely pushed a button there, Phoebe thought. Too bad she didn't yet understand what it was. "And what is the truth, Nick?" she asked. *Keep him talking,* she commanded herself. Not just Cole's life could depend on what Phoebe was able to learn from Nick. There was also the small matter of her own.

"Isn't it obvious?" Nick demanded, his expression triumphant, as if Phoebe's question had provided the opportunity he'd been hoping for. "Love is a lie. Cole had everything, when he was a demon. *Everything.* And what did he trade it in for? Nothing. There's no such thing as love."

"That's not true," Phoebe protested at once. "You're wrong."

Nick threw back his head and laughed. The sound was bitter and filled with pain. Phoebe wondered if he knew how much.

"Don't be naive. Of course it is. You think I don't know an illusion when I see one? But then you don't really know me yet, do you? You keep calling me Nick, but that's just my outer form. Yes, I was once a man named Nicolas Gerrard. But now, I'm so much more, and I owe it all to love."

Nick performed an elaborate, formal bow. "Allow me to introduce myself," he said. "I am *Tauschung*. I *am* illusion. There's nothing about lies, about illusion, that I don't know. That's how I know that's all love is. And you're going to help me prove it, Phoebe.

"Your betrayal will be the last thing Cole experiences before he dies."

Chapter

12

"Okay," Piper said. She rubbed her hands together in nervous anticipation. "We've got everything we need. We're all set, right?"

"Right," Paige affirmed.

"Set," Leo agreed.

Both nodded solemnly and took a step closer to the table in the attic on which Piper had laid out the items needed for the scrying spell. There was no reason that the spell had to be performed in the attic, but it was often the place Piper preferred. Particularly when she was attempting something she'd never done before.

The Book of Shadows was kept in the attic, a thing that made Piper feel more connected to her witch-history. And it had the added benefit of being secluded. She couldn't afford to be interrupted in the middle of the most important scrying spell she'd ever performed by having some door-to-door salesman ring the bell.

In previous scrying spells, Piper had been looking for information on demon location in the world above. The everyday world she inhabited with her sisters and husband. In those instances, she'd often utilized objects such as city maps in her spell. But since Cole was no longer a demon, and would be traveling in places for which no map existed, Piper had decided on a more . . . elemental approach.

"All right," she said, pulling in a deep breath. "Cole should be at the graveyard by now. I say it's time to get this show on the road. The sooner we start, the sooner we get Phoebe back home where she belongs."

"Absolutely, Paige agreed.

"Okay," Piper said. "Here goes."

She stepped up to the table, instinctively aligning herself along its center. Paige and Leo flanked her on either side. With both hands, Piper lifted her favorite earthenware bread-rising bowl from the table. Once, it had belonged to Gram. She had brought it back to San Francisco following a trip to the East Coast. It had come from the oldest operating pottery outlet in the country, and was made of the strong soil of the state of Vermont.

I sure hope this works, Piper thought.

In her desire to see what went on in the underworld, Piper had decided to call upon the four elements for her scrying spell. They were present everywhere, even in the underworld. Even evil needed them for its existence. The elements were the essence of existence itself. The bowl was her stand-in for the first element she would call upon. "Earth!" Piper said aloud.

She set the bowl back in the center of the table. "Water!" Piper cried.

Beside her, Leo poured a stream of clear mineral water into the earthenware bowl.

If the people who bottle Evian only knew, Piper thought. "Fire," she called.

On her other side, Paige struck a match and lit a tall, white taper. The tang of sulfur stung Piper's nostrils. She was pleased to note the candle flame burned straight and pure.

Now, there was only one element left. "Air!" Piper cried.

Together, she and Paige leaned over the bowl and blew gently across its surface, causing tiny ripples to form. Piper began to feel a pressure building behind her eyes. The back of her neck tingled, the way it did before an electrical storm. The air of the attic felt hot and close.

Now Piper repeated her call, weaving the four elements into her scrying spell.

> *"Earth, water, fire, air,*
> *Aid me in this task I dare.*
> *Where Cole wanders, let me see.*
> *As I will, so mote it be!"*

• • •

As they'd previously agreed, the exact moment Piper finished speaking, Paige plunged the lighted candle into the water just as Piper herself released Cole's cufflink into the water-filled bowl. There was a sharp *hiss* as the candle flame was extinguished. A single spiral of smoke curled upward. Just for an instant, Piper caught a glimpse of the cufflink on its journey to the bowl's bottom.

Then, without warning, the surface of the water turned an inky black. The water began to roil and thrash, like a lake in the grip of some terrific storm. The table on which the bowl rested began to vibrate, reminding Piper of a special effect in a movie séance. The air in the attic grew so close, she could feel sweat trickling down between her shoulder blades.

Then, as quickly as it had begun, the disturbance was over. The surface of the water evened out, became flat and calm, clear once more. Piper bent over it, staring into its depths. Her own reflection gazed steadily back.

Nothing, she thought desperately.

She looked up to meet Leo's eyes.

"Keep watching," he encouraged her, his voice low.

Piper returned her attention to the water. In the space of time it had taken her to look away, then back, the very substance of the water seemed to have altered. Now, it played tricks on her eyes. Still fluid, but somehow also made up of layers. How many, Piper couldn't even begin to tell. Within their depths, images floated, blurry and unfocused. Slowly at first, then moving more quickly, as if they were beginning to coalesce literally before Piper's very eyes.

I did it. It's working after all, she thought.

Abruptly, the images snapped into focus, as if some cosmic hand had just adjusted its camera lens. Beside her, Piper heard Paige suck in a breath.

"There he is!" Paige said. "I can see him! There's Cole."

Cole stood in the graveyard, clutching the kazoo in one hand. If he'd felt more ridiculous, he couldn't remember when.

He figured his own humiliation had to be part of *Tauschung's* plan. It was the quest equivalent of wrong-footing your opponent in tennis. Or making the runner stumble right out of the starting gate.

It was pretty hard to take yourself seriously when you had to summon your guide to the underworld not with something bold and daring like a trumpet, but with an instrument that made a sound that could pretty much only be described as the world's biggest raspberry.

Get over it, Cole told himself. *This is hardly the time to get all macho about your image.*

He put the kazoo to his lips and made the loudest sound he could.

The noise startled a flock of crows. They flew shrieking into the air, the graveyard ringing with the sound of their wings and their harsh, raucous calls.

When the sky cleared, Cole was no longer alone.

Standing in front of him was the oldest man he'd ever seen. He appeared so ancient, even Cole, who'd seen many things, didn't even want to hazard a guess as to how old he was. The old man was dressed in a homespun shirt, coarsely woven trousers, and sandals. His back was bent and his hands were curled, as if from the eons he'd spent plying a pair of oars.

Charon, the ferryman—whose duty was to transport newly departed souls to the realm of the dead. From his withered-apple face burned eyes as sharp and clear as a twenty-year-old's. They gazed avidly at his surroundings, then came to rest on Cole.

"My first glimpse in centuries of the world of the living," he said in a voice as dry as chalk dust, "and where do I end up? In a graveyard."

Cole mastered a sudden impulse to roar with helpless, frustrated laughter. Apparently, the universe had a sense of humor. Too bad neither he nor Charon seemed to appreciate the joke.

"Sorry," he said. "That's probably my fault. I guess I figured this was the place you'd be most comfortable."

Charon's craggy eyebrows shot straight up.

"All I ever see are dead people. A little variety might have been nice. Of course, as far as I can tell, *you're* still among the living, so I suppose you count. What's the op?"

"It's a rescue mission," Cole said. "My girlfriend's in the underworld, and I've got to get her out."

Charon shook his head. "Orpheus complex, huh? Too bad. You look like an okay guy. I don't suppose it will do any good to mention that not even Orpheus himself managed to pull off what you're proposing?"

"When I leave the underworld, I won't look back. You can trust me on that one," answered Cole. "Besides, I'm not the only one who's still alive—Phoebe is too. She's being held against her will."

"Oh well, that's different," Charon said. "Not that it necessarily improves your odds. Once somebody—living or dead—has entered the underworld, it's pretty hard to get back out. Unless you're a demon, of course. Those guys are always zapping in and out."

"I know all that," Cole said, striving to keep his tone patient. He couldn't afford to alienate his guide, his only access to Phoebe.

Charon cocked his head. "I think you do," he said thoughtfully. His bright, young eyes considered Cole. "You're the one, aren't you?" he asked after a moment.

"The one what?"

"The one everybody's talking about. You're the guy who used to be a demon but gave up his powers for love. That pissed off all sorts of things where we're headed, let me tell you."

"I know."

Charon cocked his head. "Still sure you want to go?"

"Absolutely," said Cole.

"You're in an awfully big hurry to meet your doom," Charon observed.

"Wrong," Cole answered shortly. "I'm in an awfully big hurry to rescue the woman I love. I know they're waiting for me. I'm going anyway. End of story. Can we go now?"

"Whoa," Charon said. His eyes took on an expression Cole could have sworn was amusement.

"You *have* got it bad, boy. An Orpheus complex, combined with a hero complex, with maybe a little death wish thrown in on the side. Pretty impressive. I've never ferried one of you across before. I take it back. You just might stand a chance. With a little help from your friends. Always assuming that you have some."

"I do," said Cole.

"Glad to hear it," Charon said. He grinned suddenly, exposing a set of perfect white teeth. "To tell you the truth, I'd love to see those demons taken down a notch," he confided. "They're always giving the underworld a bad name. Okay, sonny. You tell me all about who's got your sweetheart on our little trip, and I'll see if I can ferry you to a place that'll spike his guns. Nothing in the rule book says I can't do that."

Cole felt a second surge of hope. This was just the sort of thing a demon would never do: help another being with no obvious benefit to itself. But it was a very human thing to do, Cole realized suddenly. Maybe, even in the underworld, being human wasn't going to be such a disadvantage after all. "Thanks," he said.

"Don't mention it," said Charon. "You got the fare? I don't do this for free, you know."

Cole extracted the penny from his pocket and flipped it to the ferryman. Charon examined it, then made a face. "Same as always," he commented, his tone morose. "Not one raise in all these years, can you believe it? Not even a cost-of-living increase."

"I guess it's an occupational hazard of working with the dead," Cole said.

Charon threw back his head and gave a bark of laughter. "Good one. I could definitely learn to like you, sonny. You all set?"

Ready as I'll ever be, Cole thought, as he nodded.

"Okay, let's go," said Charon.

"No!" Phoebe said, her tone vehement. "No, Nick. You're wrong. I'd never betray Cole."

"Not Nick," he corrected. "Nick Gerrard was just a man. Now, I am *Tauschung*. I suggest you get used to it. Just like you ought to get used to the fact that you're going to be here for a while. And, for the record, Phoebe, you've betrayed Cole already. How else do you think you ended up here?"

"Because of your sneaky, underhanded little trick. Your *illusion*," Phoebe all but shouted. "That doesn't count. It's not the same thing, and you know it. I'd never betray Cole knowingly."

"We'll see, won't we?" *Tauschung* said, with a smug look on his face Phoebe definitely longed to wipe right off. She clenched her fists at her sides.

"Speaking of which . . . you'd like to see him, wouldn't you? You'd like to watch Cole make his doomed rescue attempt. Oh, yes," *Tauschung* went on, when, in spite of herself, Phoebe made a stricken sound. "He's coming for you. In fact, he ought to be on his way right about . . . *now!*"

He made a sudden gesture. Phoebe jumped as the candles went out. Before her eyes could adjust to the darkness, the thick red curtains hanging between the candelabrum began to glow. Then, to Phoebe's astonishment, they parted, exactly like a set of theater curtains.

He's literally setting the stage, she thought. As if she and Cole were enacting a play for his amusement. The thought made her already hot blood threaten to boil. Watching Cole fight for his life was not her idea of entertainment.

Phoebe kept her eyes on what she couldn't

help but think of as the stage. For a moment, all was dark. Then, as Phoebe continued to watch, the stage began to fill with mist.

The fog, she thought. What better medium to set the mood for an illusion? All sorts of things were starting to make sense, now. None of them good. And all of them tied to the being who insisted she call him *Tauschung.*

He made a second gesture and the mist began to settle, hovering just above the ground. Then, through the darkness, Phoebe began to distinguish figures. Two men, in a small rowboat. Though their backs were toward her, Phoebe could tell that one man was old, and the other was young.

The old man was hunched over a pair of oars. In spite of his age, his pull on them was steady and strong. The young man knelt in the bow of the rowboat, peering forward, as if trying to see where they were going.

Then it seemed to Phoebe that the younger man spoke and, as he did so, he turned around. Phoebe's heart gave a great leap as she recognized his features.

Cole, she thought. *Cole!*

Thank God he was coming for her.

Why on earth hadn't he stayed safe at home?

Chapter

13

"It's working!" Paige cried excitedly. "Piper, it's working! There he is. There's Cole." She leaned over the bowl, her face close to the water.

"Be careful, Paige. If you touch the water, you'll break the spell," Leo warned.

"Right. Okay. Sorry," Paige said as she straightened up. She put her hands behind her back, like a schoolgirl caught sneaking a treat from the cookie jar. "I guess I got kind of carried away there, for a moment. But I mean—there he is! There's Cole! That's a good sign for our side, right?"

"Right," Piper said. Now that the spell had succeeded, she realized how exhausted she was. *Leo was right,* she thought. Scrying into the underworld took enormous reserves of energy.

All the more reason to keep the energy she still had right where it belonged. "I'm excited too,

Truth and Consequences 125

sweetie," she told Paige. "But I think we all need to calm down and stay focused on Cole. That way, we'll be able to help when he needs us."

"You're right. Okay, I know you're right," Paige said. "But I just have to say one thing."

"What?"

Paige put an arm around Piper's shoulders and gave her a swift, hard squeeze. "You are totally awesome."

"We," Piper said as she returned Paige's embrace. "You mean *we*."

There might have been moments early in their relationship when she'd doubted Paige's ability to take her new responsibilities seriously, but she was coming through in the big time crunch, no two ways about it.

Sisters, Piper thought. *Now and always.*

Through the sudden tears that threatened to obscure her vision, Piper kept her eyes fixed on the water, on the image of the man who would reunite her and the sister who stood at her side with the one who had been stolen from them all.

"How much longer?" Cole asked. From his position at the bow of the rowboat, he turned to face Charon.

The first part of the trip had been taken up with the explanation of who had taken Phoebe and why. It hadn't taken all that long, but that hadn't stopped Cole from hoping they'd be wherever they were going by now. The knowledge that Phoebe was being held against her will was like a sickness, eating him from the inside out.

"We get there when we get there," the ferryman answered calmly, though his tone was sympathetic. "If you were one of my usual passengers, I'd tell you the length of the journey, not to mention the place where we land, is determined by the life you've led. With you, that doesn't exactly apply."

Cole made a frustrated sound. *What is it about supernatural good guys?* he wondered. They always seemed to talk in crypto-speak. Even Leo did that sometimes. "Sorry I asked," he muttered. "Though I'm thinking that's part of the point."

Charon grinned. "You catch on quickly."

Cole turned back around and gazed out across the water. He'd never seen anything like the water through which he and Charon were traveling. It was perfectly smooth. Absolutely dark. Not even the passage of the boat seemed to disturb it. And it reflected back nothing. Not even Cole's own face as he bent over it. Experimentally, he reached down.

"I wouldn't, if I were you," Charon said.

Cole pulled his hand up right before it touched the water. "Why not?"

Charon shrugged. "Some things are simply meant to be left alone. Besides, this place wasn't exactly designed for the living."

"What is this place exactly?" asked Cole. "I mean, I know the myth. The River Styx. But that's not all there is to this place, is there? I can feel it. There's something . . . more."

"Very good," Charon answered. "Not many of my passengers get that, but then they do have other things on their minds. To put it simply, this is the void. The space between the world above and the world below. You probably didn't even notice it, when you were a demon. Those guys zap right through it. Besides, for demons, the void is just another place. It isn't really important.

"But, for mortals, it's a different story. The void is the transition, the place where they first come face-to-face with the fact that they're not in Kansas anymore. The boat and the water, they're just trappings. Things to make the passage more user-friendly, you might say."

"What about you?" Cole inquired, studying Charon a little more closely. He was intrigued in spite of the urgency of his situation, he had to admit.

"I'm the same way," Charon nodded. "You might say I'm the face of the void. Now, don't get me wrong. We exist, my boat and me. We're real enough. But so is the void. We have a sort of mutually beneficial arrangement. An eternal status quo. I don't mess with the void; the void doesn't mess with me. So I'd appreciate it if you'd keep your hands inside the boat, sonny. Your presence here is disturbance enough."

"Because I'm alive, you mean," said Cole.

Charon nodded. "And because of who you

are. You may not be a demon any longer, but you have a fair amount of power, you know. That choice you made really stirred things up."

Abruptly, for no reason Cole could see, Charon shifted his pull on the oars. The boat began to move at a different angle.

"Almost there now," the ferryman said.

"Where will you set me down?" asked Cole.

"In the place they're least likely to monitor. Not that it will be a walk in the park. But coincidentally, it's not very far from where your pal *Tauschung*'s settled down. Kind of interesting, that."

"What?" asked Cole.

"He's pretty anxious to prove he's as bad a boy as any of the demons, but he can't escape what he is, no matter how hard he tries. Still, I suppose the same could be said of all of us."

"Some more than others," Cole said.

Charon grinned. "I guess you'd know. You'll still want to watch your back after I set you down, though," the ferryman went on. "Things where you're going can get a little unpredictable."

"Already part of the plan," said Cole.

Without warning, he pitched forward, bracing himself as the boat encountered something solid.

"Okay, this is it," said Charon.

Cole gazed forward. *Figures,* he thought. He couldn't see a thing. "You're sure about this?" he asked.

Again, the ferryman grinned. "Trust me. The second your feet touch the soil of the underworld, you'll be able to find your way. You can't see anything now because you're still a part of the void. Just step out of the boat and you'll be all set."

Cole extended one hand. After a moment, Charon took it. The old man's grasp was firm and sure, though his hands were the coldest things that Cole had ever felt. As the handshake broke up, Cole was startled to see that there were tears in the other man's eyes.

"Good luck," Charon said gruffly.

"Thanks," Cole said. He turned back around. Cautiously, he rose to his feet, balancing in the rowboat. "All I have to do is step out, huh?"

"That'll do it," Charon confirmed. "Though, there is a little something you could do for me, if you want."

"What's that?" asked Cole, as he turned to face Charon one last time.

"You can nail those scum-sucking girlfriend snatchers right to the wall."

"I'll do my best," Cole promised.

"Excellent," Charon said. "Well, don't just stand there, sonny. She's waiting for you, isn't she? Get going."

Cole turned around. He lifted his leg, extended it, set his foot down. Relief coursed through his body when his foot encountered something solid.

"Remember," he heard Charon's voice say. "Don't look back. Look forward."

"I'll remember," Cole promised. Then he lifted his other foot and brought it down alongside the first. Both feet were now firmly planted on the soil of the underworld. He could almost hear a door slam shut at his back. He knew better than to do so, but Cole was certain if he turned around, there'd be no sign of Charon.

For a moment, Cole stood perfectly still, doing nothing more than breathing in and out. Then, just as Charon had promised, the underworld slowly began to emerge around him. It wasn't that things really grew any brighter. This portion of the underworld seemed to exist in a state of perpetual gloom. It was more that, the longer Cole stood, the more he gained the ability to make sense of the darkness.

Cole knelt down. Scooping up a handful of soil, he let it trickle out between his fingers.

Sand, he thought. He knew where Charon had delivered him, now. A place even demons knew to avoid.

The Wasteland.

To reach Phoebe, Cole would have to cross it.

Well, no time like the present, he thought. He straightened up. Lifting one foot, Cole set it down, waiting until he was sure it would bear his weight before he did the same with the other. Cole had no idea how long it would take him to cross the Wasteland. It didn't matter, so he didn't bother thinking about it. What mattered was that Phoebe was somewhere on the other side. That meant Cole would walk until he came to the Wasteland's end, or drop in his tracks trying.

He began to move in a slow, steady rhythm, conserving his strength, pacing himself.

Hold on, Phoebe, he thought. *I'm coming.*

Chapter

14

The Power of Darkness was not a happy camper.

"What do you mean he's here?" he snarled to the minion who cowered before him. "If he's here, why hasn't he been brought before me?"

The demon minion mumbled something incomprehensible. His snout was pressed against the ground, a thing that made him more difficult than usual to understand.

"Oh, get up!" the Power of Darkness snapped. He waved one arm, sending the demon flying backward through the air and out into the nearest corridor. There was a juicy *splat* as the minion's airborne journey ended at the wall.

The Power of Darkness paid no attention. Muttering angrily to himself, he strode across the room to a brazier. With his bare hand, he reached in and stirred up the coals. Then he took up a handful of black powder and tossed it over them. At once, an acrid smoke rose up and hovered in the air, as if waiting for instructions.

The Power of Darkness was happy to oblige.

There were a number of things he very much wanted to know—starting with why the one servant who should have informed him of Cole's arrival had failed to do so.

"Show me *Tauschung*," the Power of Darkness roared.

"He did it. He made it," Piper said. She swayed a little, as her relief literally made her light-headed. "Way to go, Cole."

"So, now he just needs to find Phoebe, right?" Paige put in.

"Right," Piper confirmed. *To say nothing of avoiding whatever traps the demons dream up,* she added silently, but chose not to say aloud. There'd been something about the tone of Paige's voice. A little too bright. A little too hopeful.

She's feeling the strain already, Piper thought. And they'd barely gotten started. For Cole, and for all of them, there was still a long way to go.

The image the scrying spell revealed showed that Cole was moving slowly but steadily across what appeared to be a vast desert. As she watched Cole's progress, Piper felt a great wave of weariness sweep over her. She swayed again, gripping the table edge in an attempt to steady herself. Instantly, she felt Leo's supporting arm at her back.

"What's wrong, Piper?"

Piper shook her head, trying to clear it. "I'm not sure," she admitted after a moment. "I felt sort of light-headed for a second there. Now, all I feel is tired. It's like I've been walking for miles."

"I was afraid something like this might happen," Leo said. "I think it's a side effect of the scrying spell."

Piper leaned her head back against Leo's chest, which made her feel much better. "I've never experienced these kinds of side effects before."

"You've never tried scrying in the underworld," Leo reminded. "That's draining enough. But I think what you're feeling is because the spell has somehow tied you to Cole."

"You mean, as if I'm experiencing what he does?" Piper asked.

She lifted her head from Leo's chest and stared down at the images of Cole. He was struggling up a steep rise. Fit as he was, his breathing was labored. When he reached the top, he halted, bent over at the waist, his hands on his knees as he struggled to catch his breath. Though her breathing was definitely easier, Piper felt a corresponding burn in her lungs.

"Yes," answered Leo. "Not to the same extent, obviously. But I do think there's a link."

"Does it go both ways?" Paige asked suddenly. "I mean—can Piper, you know, send Cole positive energy, or something?"

Leo shook his head. "I don't think so. Piper's scrying spell is drawing energy out of the underworld, toward her, not the other way around. Cole is the conduit, the focal point. The energy is being channeled through him. Whatever danger he encounters could endanger Piper too."

"Great. Just what we needed," Piper muttered.

"Where *is* Cole, Leo?" Paige asked. "Do you know?"

"I think so," Leo answered. "It's called the Wasteland."

"And what is that, exactly?" Piper inquired.

"Pretty much what the name implies," Leo replied. "The dead who inhabit it come to be there because they literally wasted their lives. They had the chance to do good, to make a difference, and let it pass them by. After death, they're sent to the Wasteland. A place where all they can do is reflect on the barrenness of their former lives."

"That's why it looks like a desert," Paige said, making the connection.

Leo nodded. "That's right."

"So what will they do when they see someone living?" Piper wondered aloud.

"Good question," Leo replied. "There's really no way to know. They could help Cole, as a way of making atonement. They could just as easily try to destroy him. Or, they could be so wrapped up in their own misery that they don't even notice he's there at all. It's impossible to predict. The Wasteland is pretty much a wild card. All we can do is keep watching and hope for the best."

"He's starting to move again," Paige said, pointing to the image of Cole. He'd pushed himself upright and was starting back down the slope.

Just for a moment, Piper closed her eyes. She was tired, so tired. And if what she felt was a fraction of what Cole was feeling . . .

It's hopeless, she thought. And felt Paige's hand on her shoulder.

"It'll be all right, Piper," Paige said softly. "Even if Cole can't feel it, we've got to keep our energy strong. We've got to keep it positive."

Piper opened her eyes. Paige was right, she thought. She had to be strong, she had to think positive.

You can do it, Cole, she thought. We *can do it*.

They could find Phoebe, and bring her back home.

Chapter

15

"The Wasteland," *Tauschung* remarked. "Now that's a surprise. And Charon deciding to help him—I didn't see that one coming either, I must admit. This could be even more . . . interesting than I anticipated."

Oh great, Phoebe thought. *'Cause it's been so dull so far.* Still, anything that came as a surprise to *Tauschung* had to be considered a plus for team Charmed Ones.

"You know us humans," she remarked aloud. "Or maybe you don't. Seeing as how you're so interested in convincing me you're much *more* than human. We're full of surprises." Phoebe gave *Tauschung* a cheeky grin, one that displayed a lot of teeth. "Just a friendly little reminder."

"I wouldn't get your hopes up, Phoebe," *Tauschung* said, almost as if he'd read her mind.

His voice was calm, but Phoebe noticed the way the color came into his cheeks as he turned from the image of Cole struggling across the Wasteland to face her.

There's . . . something, she thought. Something about the way Nick, *Tauschung*, felt about his humanity, or lack thereof. What had he said before? That he wanted to teach Cole a lesson. Prove to him the choice he'd made had been the wrong one.

Her silent-treatment tactic was starting to pay off, Phoebe realized. The longer Nick talked, the more he revealed. Now she just had to hope she could get him to reveal enough.

"So Cole made a friend, and the friend did him a favor," *Tauschung* went on. "Big deal. It's not going to make any difference in the long run."

"You don't know that," Phoebe countered.

"You're right, I don't," *Tauschung* agreed, his tone suspiciously pleasant. "But let's try a little exercise in hope versus logic, shall we? Assuming the things in the Wasteland don't get him first, Cole's still got to locate you, then get the two of you out of the underworld alive.

"How likely do you think that is? Half the demons down here would like nothing better than to tear him to pieces. The other half will be happy to take care of you. I'd say those are pretty steep odds."

"*Your* odds," Phoebe said, though it was hard to prevent the swift clutch of fear around her heart. Much as she hated to admit it, *Tauschung* was right: Things didn't look good.

But isn't that what hope is for? Phoebe wondered suddenly. *Isn't hope the thing that gives you the power to keep on going, even in the face of impossible odds?* As long as she continued to hope, there *was* hope. For her, and for Cole.

"I've always had this problem with logic," she confessed, determined to do whatever she could to spike *Tauschung*'s guns. *Keep him distracted,* she thought. *Keep him talking.* Besides, there was something about his tone, his expression. So smug. So certain. The truth was, it pissed Phoebe off. Made her long to take him down a notch. At least.

Nothing's over till it's over, she thought. *And this isn't over yet. Not by a long shot.*

"The thing about logic is that it works best in a vacuum," she went on. "*Logically,* I would think the trouble with that would be pretty obvious. It fails to take the unexpected into account. Take Charon helping Cole. There was no logical reason for that to have happened, but it did. If the unexpected happened once, it can happen again. I'd say that changes your odds."

Tauschung's eyes narrowed. It was obvious the conversation wasn't going quite the way he'd wished. "Poor Phoebe," he said. "You're grasping at straws."

You'd like to think so, wouldn't you? Phoebe thought. *You think you have me penned. . . . Well, get ready. I am going to rattle your cage, pal.*

She began to stroll around the room, toying with the rich objects with which it was decorated, deliberately paying no attention to the images of Cole. Much as she wanted to monitor his progress, Phoebe was rapidly coming to the conclusion that she couldn't afford to. Watching Cole kept her passive, reminded her she was a prisoner and helpless. Probably exactly what *Tauschung* had in mind.

"Where I come from, we call it the power of positive thinking," she said as she picked up a delicate china shepardess and turned it over in her hands. "Not grasping at straws. Things are just getting started around here, *Nick*. Unless seeing into the future is part of your bag of tricks, not even you know how they'll turn out. I'd stop counting your demons before they're zapped, if I were you."

Tauschung took a step toward her, then checked himself. "But Cole can't do any zapping anymore, can he?" he asked, the taunt plain in his voice. "That's part of the problem. Nothing, no matter how unexpected, can alter the fact that he's human. *Only* human."

Oh, yeah. That is definitely the key, Phoebe thought. In spite of the long odds against her, she could feel her excitement rising. The more Nick talked, the shorter the odds became.

"Maybe you ought to give being human a little more credit," she observed. "There's more to us than meets the eye. I wouldn't have thought I'd need to explain a concept like that to you. But then I suppose tunnel vision is always a danger when all you do is think about yourself."

"Oh, right," *Tauschung* said, his tone heavy with sarcasm. "And the fact that you think about Cole, that you *love* him, makes you so strong. You've got it backward, Phoebe. Love splits your focus. It brings confusion. Love makes you weak, not strong. You don't believe me? Look at Cole. His love for you brought him back to the underworld, the very last place he should have chosen. Now he's in mortal danger. Literally.

"Why? Because of his love for you. That's the thing that will bring him down."

No! Phoebe thought as the china shepardess slipped from her fingers and fell to the table with a *clunk*.

With every fiber of her being, Phoebe rejected *Tauschung*'s argument. It wasn't that she was blind. She could see his point. It was simply that she refused to believe it. Refused to believe that love was a destructive force.

In spite of herself, Phoebe felt her eyes pulled back to the images of Cole, to the images of the man who loved her. The man to whom she'd pledged her love. He was moving across what looked to be an enormous desert. Phoebe could see the weariness in Cole's face.

"That's right, Phoebe," *Tauschung* murmured. "Watch the man you love. Watch Cole. See his pain and suffering? That's just the beginning. There'll be more, much, much more before the end. And all of it because of love. That's what love *is*, Phoebe."

"No," Phoebe whispered. "I don't believe you." *I won't believe you. Cole!* she thought. *Cole!*

As she continued to watch, Cole stumbled, then fell to his knees. Phoebe's heart leaped into her throat. But Cole simply pushed himself to his feet and kept on going. As she focused on his face, Phoebe became aware of something that hadn't been obvious before. A thing she wondered if *Tauschung* noticed.

Cole's face was etched with weariness, it was true. But just beneath it was something else. Determination. No matter what happened, Cole would never give up. Not just because he was stubborn, though he certainly was that, but because he had something to sustain him through his challenges.

That's what love is, Phoebe thought as all the doubts that had risen up to plague her abruptly vanished. For a moment, she'd let her fears get the better of her. But Cole himself had helped to prove that *Tauschung* really did have it wrong.

Love wasn't the thing that brought on pain and suffering. It was the thing that saw you through them. *Like hope,* Phoebe thought. As if love and hope were two points of a triangle. Two points of another power of three—one any two people could create together.

And the third point was the hardest to accomplish, she realized suddenly as the concept she was forming crystalized in her mind. More difficult to master than love or hope. Those were things you could do without thinking, almost by instinct, the impulse rising straight up from the gut.

But the third power required something extra: a combination of instinct and conscious thought. It required you to look yourself square in the face, acknowledge your fears, and then relinquish them.

The third point of the triangle was trust.

That's where she and Cole had broken down, Phoebe thought. They'd forgotten to trust. In so doing, they'd opened a door. Through it had stepped the Power of Darkness and his henchman, *Tauschung*. Together, they had driven a wedge between Cole and Phoebe. A wedge that now threatened their very lives, and more.

If Phoebe remained in the underworld, the magical Power of Three would be broken. Her sisters would be in mortal danger forever, hampered in their ability to protect both the innocents who needed them and themselves.

And all because of words spoken in hurt and anger. Because, in their hurt and anger, Phoebe and Cole had forgotten to trust.

Looks like I'll just have to kick the wedge out and

slam the door shut, won't I? Phoebe thought. *Make the triangle whole once more.* There was no time like the present when it came to getting started. Particularly as neither she nor Cole had all that much time.

Ruthlessly, Phoebe pulled her eyes away from the images of Cole, and turned them back to *Tauschung*.

Time to up the ante on turning the tables, she thought. He'd tried for her weak spot and failed. Now it was her turn.

But before she could begin, he spoke. "It's starting to happen, isn't it, Phoebe?" he asked. "You know Cole's going to fail, and it's getting harder and harder to watch. You want to look away. I understand that. It's only natural when you look on something horrible."

"You're wrong, *Nick*," she said, emphasizing his human name and at the same time being careful to keep her voice calm and quiet. Deliberately, she shifted her eyes to Cole and let them remain there as she went on. "I'm not afraid to face the truth, but I think you are."

"I don't know what you mean," he said at once. "And I've told you before, my name is *Tauschung*."

"I think you do," Phoebe said. Just as deliberately as she'd turned her attention to Cole, she shifted her eyes back to Nick's face. *You are not in control here, pal,* she thought.

"Someone once hurt you very badly, didn't

she?" she asked quietly. "So badly, you decided it was safer not to be human. So you became a pawn of the Power of Darkness. I'd say that makes love pretty strong, wouldn't you?"

Quick, hot color flooded Nick's face. Pain. Embarrassment. Fury. Which it was, Phoebe couldn't tell, but she could tell that it was almost overwhelming.

"What is this?" Nick asked, his voice rough with the strain of keeping his emotions under control. "*Psych 101?* Not that I don't appreciate the effort. But it's just a little obvious, don't you think?"

"That doesn't make it any less true," Phoebe replied. "All those funny stories you told me at dinner that night, about how all those women had broken up with you, I know that they were lies. But somewhere in your past is the truth, *Nick*. The story you're afraid to tell. The one that made you turn away from love."

Nick laughed, and the sound was bitter. Abruptly, he sat down in his chair, his back to the images of Cole, as if the pleasure of watching his adversary struggle had suddenly lost all its appeal.

"Oh, Phoebe," he said, his tone weary. "You think you've got it all worked out, when actually, you've got it all wrong. I didn't turn away from love. It turned away from me. Literally. All right, yes, I loved a woman once. And she loved me, or so I thought.

"It turned out it was my possessions and my

face she loved. I lost them both to the revolutionaries who burned my family's château to the
ground. When my 'true love' saw what the fire
had done to my face, she couldn't bear the sight
of it. *She turned away.* Rejected me, rejected the
thing I had become. And so I decided to become
something else. A thing no woman would have
the power to reject, ever again."

"Illusion," Phoebe murmured as, suddenly, it
all began to make horrible sense. "*Tauschung.*"

Nick nodded, his weary expression changing
to one that was defiant and proud. Almost as if
he was daring Phoebe to prove the choice he'd
made had been the wrong one.

Phoebe never knew what inspired her to ask
the question. But as soon as she did, she knew it
was the right one. "What about you, Nick? What
do you see when you look at yourself?"

Nick flinched, as if she'd struck him. "You ask
too many questions," he said.

"You can't do it, can you?" Phoebe asked, the
inspiration carrying her along like a tide. "You
can't face yourself."

Nick started from his seat so suddenly,
Phoebe jolted back.

"And you think you can?" he yelled. "You
have no idea what I am, no idea what you're
dealing with, Phoebe Halliwell."

"I think I do," Phoebe countered, though her
heart was pounding. One part of her urged her to
press home her advantage, while the other

warned her to hold back. Phoebe took the first choice.

"There's a name for someone who can't face himself," she said. "You know it as well as I do: *coward*. You think joining the underworld made you stronger, don't you? It didn't. All it did was give you a darker place to hide."

"You want to see me, is that it?" Nick said, his voice like the crack of a whip. "Is that what you want? Be careful what you wish for, Phoebe. You just might get it."

"Talk, talk, talk," Phoebe said as adrenaline surged through her body. "But no action. Why is that, I wonder? Oh, wait. I know. It's because you're afraid I can do something you can't, isn't it?"

Nick gave an ugly laugh. "Not likely."

"Prove it," Phoebe challenged.

There was a beat of silence. Across it, Nick and Phoebe stared at each other. Green eyes locked with brown. Then, slowly, Nick began to smile. "Very well," he said. "You think you're stronger than I am, then *you* prove it. But just remember, you asked for this."

Phoebe felt a pulse of energy move through the room like a wave of static electricity. There was a crackle, and a hiss. The room was plunged into total darkness. "That's a little theatrical, don't you think?" she inquired, though her heart was pounding. "Besides, it's hard to terrify me into submission when I can't see a thing."

Silence.

Phoebe felt a tingle slide down the back of her neck. "Nick?" she called out.

Again, there was nothing. No light. No sound, save for the pounding of Phoebe's own heart. Then, with the same abruptness with which all lights had vanished, the candles in the candelabrum suddenly flared to life. Behind them, the red curtains were closed once more. Cole was nowhere to be seen.

Neither was Nick Gerrard.

At the exact moment he'd been about to reveal himself to Phoebe, something had intervened. She was pretty sure she knew what it was.

The Power of Darkness.

Why didn't it take me, too? she wondered. Was Nick's—*Tauschung's*—sudden disappearance a part of his plan? Or had the unexpected happened once again, in spite of all his logical odds?

Beats me, Phoebe thought.

But there was one thing she knew for certain. She was not about to stand around and wait to find out. Her captor was gone. That meant she could be too.

Her decision made, Phoebe sprang into action at once. She moved swiftly toward the door of the chamber, coming to rest with her back flat against the wall. Then, pulling in a steadying breath, Phoebe thrust her head out into the corridor, did a quick survey, then whipped it back again.

Nothing.

No alarms had gone off when she'd stuck some portion of her body outside the room. There were no demons of any shape, size, or description guarding the corridor. Unless, of course, they were of the invisible variety. But that didn't seem like *Tauschung*'s style, somehow. It was hard to be demoralized by something you couldn't see coming.

Which meant that, for the moment at least, the coast was clear. *Okay*, Phoebe thought. *Here goes nothing.*

She was going to do the thing she should have done before, but hadn't: meet Cole halfway.

On silent feet, Phoebe slipped from the room and began to make her way along the corridor. She reached a junction, hesitated a moment, and then bore left. The direction of her heart.

As she moved, she tried to still the tiny voice in her mind that jeered at her, informing her the direction she took didn't make one bit of difference.

She didn't have the faintest idea where *halfway* was.

Chapter

16

Cole's head pounded. His legs felt like rubber. His eyes stung. They were so dry, even blinking made them hurt. The inside of his mouth was as parched as the Sahara.

No doubt because the rest of him felt like he'd just walked across it.

Charon had definitely been right about one thing, Cole thought. Crossing the Wasteland bore absolutely no resemblance to a walk in the park. At least the dead who inhabited the place had left him alone. So far. Though Cole had heard them—he was sure of that. The Wasteland might not be much to look at, but, like the desert it resembled, it was full of sound.

A low moaning filled the air. Sometimes soft, sometimes loud. If he'd been anywhere but the underworld, Cole might have mistaken it for the wind. But here, he knew better. In this place, he

knew enough to recognize the sound for what
it was.

The moaning of souls in torment, unable to
rest. Cole couldn't see them, but he could hear
them and feel them all around him. Once, as he'd
topped a rise, he'd been stopped cold by sobbing
so bitter, he'd thought his heart would break.

He'd done the only thing he could: put his
hands over his ears, lifted one heavy foot, then
the other, and kept on going. The beings in this
place were beyond his help, no matter how
much he might feel for them.

But Phoebe wasn't.

Cole took another few staggering steps, his
eyes searching the distance. There it was. He
could see it now. The place that marked the end
of the first part of his journey.

It was called the Boundary and was, quite
simply, a wall of fire.

On the other side of it, somewhere, Phoebe
was being held prisoner. To reach her, Cole
would literally have to walk through fire. There
was no other way. As far as he knew, the
Boundary was endless. There was no way to
walk around. He might have tried going over
but, near the Boundary, the landscape of the
Wasteland was as flat as a pancake. Even when
he'd been a demon, Cole had hardly been able
to leap tall buildings, or tall walls of fire, with a
single bound.

To make matters even worse, Cole had no

idea how thick the Boundary was. If it was as thin as a few steps, chances were good he would make it through relatively unscathed. If it was much wider, he might as well be committing suicide. His quest for Phoebe would be over almost as soon as it had begun.

That was the not-so-good part.

In fact, the only good part of the whole situation that Cole could think of was that Charon had been right about this being the one way into *Tauschung*'s territory that wasn't guarded or watched. *Why bother? Let's face it*, Cole thought.

He continued to move forward, halting only when the heat of the Boundary grew uncomfortable. Motionless now, Cole studied the wall of fire. Even the moaning of the Wasteland seemed to die down as Cole stood still, trying to ignore the way the heat from the Boundary stung his already parched skin. Silently, he contemplated his options.

It took him all of about twenty seconds to narrow it down to three:

Go forward.

Go back.

Stay right where he was.

The second two were plainly unacceptable. That left him with option number one. *Gee*, he thought. *Now there's a surprise.* There had never really been a question about what he would do. Not as long as Phoebe was on the other side of the Boundary.

His decision made, Cole stripped off his jacket and, keeping it open, draped it over one arm. He was glad now that he hadn't given in to the temptation that had seized him in the heat of the Wasteland: to take the jacket off and leave it behind. Now, he could use it as a barrier between his head and the flames. It might not provide much protection, but he figured anything would be better than nothing.

Cole pulled in several deep breaths, ignoring the way the hot air scorched his throat. He shook out his aching legs, trying to get the blood pumping again, wishing his body didn't feel so sluggish. He was going to have to move as quickly as he could for as long as he could.

Abruptly, Charon's voice filled his mind. *Remember, don't look back. Look forward.*

Good advice, Cole thought. He'd take that as a hopeful sign. He pulled in a final deep breath, muscles already tensed to begin his sprint through the flames.

Before he could take a single step, the ground beneath his feet began to shake, and the air to moan once more, a frenzy of despairing sound. The sand began to hiss and shudder, churning like the surface of a pot of boiling water. Cole stumbled backward, desperately trying to maintain his balance.

Then, shooting up from the surface of the boiling sand like the tentacles of some outrageous octopus, they came.

Hands. Arms.

The hands of the dead. Clawing one another in their haste to get to Cole. More numerous than he could count. An endless sea of desperate, grasping appendages. Cole had time for one last horrified thought.

The dead didn't just inhabit the Wasteland. They *were* the Wasteland.

Then the hands found him, wrapped him in their strong embrace, and pulled him down, down, down. Cole struggled every inch of the way, shouting Phoebe's name as the sand reached his knees, his waist, and then his chest.

Calling her name even as the sand of the Wasteland poured into his open mouth and filled his throat.

And then, at last, even the Wasteland itself was silent.

Chapter

17

Piper crumpled to the floor.

One minute, she'd been watching Cole prepare to cross the wall of fire. Worrying about whether he could make it. The next—the truth was, Piper wasn't quite sure what had happened next. But, given Cole's location, she had to figure all hell breaking loose figured rather prominently.

It was her last coherent thought.

She could feel her connection to Cole grow tighter, like a rope abruptly snapping taut. Piper had a sudden vivid image of herself and Cole, linked together by a straining, fraying lifeline. Now, Piper was half in the world above, half below, her senses operating dimly in both.

Over the roaring in her ears, Piper could hear Paige begging Leo for help.

"What's happening?" Paige cried out. "What should I do? Tell me what to do to help."

"Calm down, Paige," Piper heard Leo say. "You can't help anybody if you panic."

That's my sweetie, Piper thought. She wished she could tell him how much she appreciated what he was doing, but she couldn't seem to find the air.

"Of course I'm panicking," Paige all but yelled. "In case you haven't noticed, we're in the middle of a crisis!"

"Keep your eyes on the water," Piper heard Leo instruct. "One of us has got to keep a watch out for Cole."

"Okay," Paige said. "Okay, I can do that."

Dimly, Piper felt Leo kneel down at her side. "Piper? Can you hear me?" he asked. He took her hand in his and squeezed it. Hard. Summoning all her energy, Piper squeezed back. But he was far away. So very far.

"She's still with us," Piper heard Leo say. "She just can't communicate very well."

"Is that a bad thing or a good thing?" Paige asked, her voice shaky with emotion.

"Both," Leo answered shortly. Piper felt him gather her up into his arms. "Any sign of Cole?" he asked Paige.

"None," Paige responded. "Should I try to orb him out?"

"Not yet," Leo said, his tone grim. "But I think we should be ready to try."

No! Piper thought. *You can't. Phoebe . . .* She began to struggle in Leo's arms.

"What's happening?" Paige demanded. "Is she having a seizure or something?"

"I don't know," Leo said. "She could be trying to tell us something, or it could be related to what Cole is experiencing."

"Like dying, you mean?" Paige inquired. Even through her dimmed senses, Piper could hear the hysteria rising in her youngest sister's voice. "You saw what those things did to him, Leo. He won't last more than a few minutes under that sand. You've got to let me orb him back."

Piper's body shuddered as she tried to pull in air. *I've got to tell them, make them understand,* she thought.

"If we bring him back now, we may lose the chance to rescue Phoebe," Leo reminded.

"Chance? What chance?" Paige began to sob. "Those things down there are trying to kill Cole, and he hasn't even made it into demon territory. If we don't do something fast, they'll succeed. The only *chance* we've got to rescue Phoebe is to try again. We won't even have that if we lose Cole. You've got to help me bring him back. *Now.* Please, Leo."

Abruptly, Leo seemed to make a decision. Gently, he laid Piper down on the floor. Piper heard the sound of his footsteps as he rose and went to stand beside Paige.

"I don't like it, but I agree with you," she heard him say. "Let's not waste any more time. Let's get him out of there."

"Thank you," breathed Paige. "Piper will be okay once we get Cole back, won't she?"

Piper is okay now, Piper thought. *I just have to find a way to tell you. . . .*

"She should be," Leo said. "Okay, ready?"

"As I'll ever be," Paige answered.

Piper summoned all her strength. *"Nooo,"* she moaned.

Paige's voice choked off. "What is it?" she cried. "What's happening to Piper?"

"The water!" Leo exclaimed. "Paige, look!"

"What on earth?" Paige asked. Hardly daring to breathe, she leaned over the scrying bowl while Leo once again knelt down beside Piper.

"I don't believe it," Paige said, just as Piper sat bolt upright, chest heaving as she pulled air into her desperately aching lungs. She began to cough, leaning against Leo for support.

"Not on earth, beneath it," she said, when she could speak.

Paige shook her head in wonder. "Through it, I think you mean. I guess it just goes to show that miracles can happen anywhere, even in the underworld."

"Spoken like a true Whitelighter," Leo said with a smile.

He was going to die. The sand was going to kill him. It was just a matter of time.

The sand was everywhere, filling Cole's eyes,

his nose, his mouth, and his ears. Working its way into his clothes to scrape against his skin. It was above him, and below him. There before him, and following after him. Wrapping itself around him like a long-lost sweetheart. Claiming him, at last, for its very own.

Cole could feel his heart beating hard and fast. Though the sand muffled the sound, there was a ringing in his ears. Dimly, he realized it emanated from inside his own body, from his head, and his desperately aching lungs.

He tried struggling against the hands that held him, forcing him through the sand like a worm through dirt, but he knew it was useless. His strength was failing. He was weak. They were strong. And there were so very, very many of them.

Some hero I turned out to be, Cole thought. *I'm sorry, Phoebe. I did my best.*

Too bad it hadn't been good enough.

Then, as suddenly as he'd been sucked down, Cole felt himself propelled upward. His head and shoulders exploded into the open air. Instantly, his instinct for survival kicked into action. His arms clawed their way upward until they reached the surface. With one arm braced against the ground, Cole steadied himself. The other hand scrabbled at his mouth, desperately trying to clear it of sand. He pulled in a ragged breath, then choked. He spat out sand and pulled in a second breath.

And then he felt the hands again. Clinging

tightly to his legs. *No!* Cole thought. *Not again!*
He'd never survive another trip under. Of that,
he was absolutely certain.

Then the hands gave a heave, and his body
shot upward.

He was out. On, not under, dry land.

Lungs pumping, Cole lay still, too exhausted
for a moment to even try to make sense of what
had happened. Then, carefully, he pushed himself upright and looked around. Even then, it
took several seconds for the truth to register.

The sand was gone. He was out of the
Wasteland, on the far side of the Boundary.

Slowly, Cole got to his feet. Around him
stretched a field of grass. As if to mock the
Wasteland's inhabitants, the land on the other
side of the Boundary was lush and green, invit-
ing as an oasis. Beside it, the fire of the Boundary
burned all the hotter, all the brighter in contrast.
Cole could feel its fierce heat from where he
stood.

I never would have made it, he realized suddenly.
There wasn't a thing that lived that could have
survived a trip through the Boundary. He knew
that now. But the inhabitants of the Wasteland
had known something Cole hadn't: There was
another way to get to the other side of the
Boundary. They'd taken Cole the only way they
could.

Not over. Not around, he thought. *But* underneath *the Boundary*.

The inhabitants of the Wasteland hadn't been trying to kill him. They'd been trying to help the only way they knew how. As if, by aiding Cole, they'd found a way to make a difference at last. A way to make amends for their wasted lives.

Cole cleared his parched and aching throat.

"I don't know if you can hear me. But—thank you," he choked out. He tried to go on, to think of some way to express all the things he felt, then realized he already had. Sometimes, the simplest words were enough.

He felt a strange motion ripple through the soil beneath his feet. Cole stared down. Gazing up through the green of the grass were eyes, hundreds and hundreds of them, stretching as far as Cole's own eyes could see. All of them fixed on him with unwavering intensity, insatiable need.

"Thank you," Cole said again. "You made a difference. I won't forget."

Cole felt the earth sigh as if, against all odds, the need had been satisfied. One by one, the eyes winked out.

Cole turned and began to make his way across the field, every step taking him closer to Phoebe, and closer to all the inhabitants of the underworld who really did want to end his life.

Chapter

18

"You owe me an explanation," the Power of Darkness said. "I intend to have it, before I end your miserable existence by ripping your head off no matter what your face looks like. I estimate my patience will last about another thirty seconds."

He glared at the wall of his chamber, where his powers had *Tauschung* pinned like a bug.

"Start talking," commanded the Power of Darkness.

Fury coursed through *Tauschung*'s veins. The trouble was, he didn't know who angered him more, Phoebe or himself. *The witch played me,* he thought. She'd made a series of lucky guesses and had gotten him to do the one thing he never did. One of the things he'd vowed he would never do again.

Lose control.

You'll pay for that, Phoebe Halliwell, he thought.

"I'm waiting," the Power of Darkness reminded.

"I'm sorry if I've offended you, Master," *Tauschung* gasped out. "But there was no need for you to intervene. I had everything under control."

"Under control!" roared the Power of Darkness. "You knew the betrayer was in the underworld, yet you did nothing, including inform me. You call that having everything under control?"

"But I wasn't doing nothing," *Tauschung* protested. "I was going according to my plan. Working on the witch's tender sensibilities, letting things unfold. I would have informed you of the betrayer's whereabouts when the time was right."

"Oh, really?" asked the Power of Darkness, and now its voice was dangerously soft. "And who are you to decide when it's the right time? I think you've forgotten which one of us is in charge around here."

Not likely, *Tauschung* thought. He'd lost all feeling in his arms. "I don't suppose it ever occurred to you to trust me," he said.

His master gave a derisive snort. "Apparently, you've also forgotten who I am," he said. "If I were you, I'd give me that explanation. *Now.*"

"You want them destroyed, they'll be destroyed," *Tauschung* promised hurriedly. "It's all in the plan, just like we discussed. But you don't want to stop with their physical bodies. Can't you see that's not enough?"

"It's a pretty good place to start," the Power of

Darkness huffed. And it was more than anyone in the underworld had actually managed to accomplish so far. "I have the betrayer. I want him dead. You know this. Why has it not been done?"

"Because the timing isn't right yet," *Tauschung* soothed. The more agitated the Power of Darkness revealed himself to be, the more *Tauschung* felt himself calm. It was time to get back in control, he thought. So he could get back to business. Finish the job. If he had to do a little ego-stroking to get the job done, fine.

"Before the betrayer can be killed, he must become the betrayed. He and his witch must be reunited. Once she's betrayed him, it won't be just their lives that you will claim. Their minds, their wills, their very *souls* will be forfeit. That's what the plan we've designed will accomplish. It will destroy them *entirely*. When it succeeds, nothing will want to stand against you, you'll be so powerful."

"And if it fails?" asked the Power of Darkness.

"But it can't fail!" *Tauschung* all but shouted. "It relies on human nature. *Their* human nature. Just let me do my work, and the betrayer and his witch will destroy themselves."

"If they don't, I'll destroy you," the Power of Darkness vowed. He waved a hand, and *Tauschung* slid down the wall to land with a *thud* on the stone floor below. As he rose painfully to his feet, there was a scratching at the chamber entrance.

"What?" the Power of Darkness barked.

A minion with a bruised face cautiously thrust its head through the open door.

"Greetings, O horrific one," he began.

"Save it," snapped the Power of Darkness. "Just tell me what I want to know."

"The betrayer has crossed the Boundary, and the witch has escaped," the minion said quickly.

The Power of Darkness grinned at *Tauschung*.

"A little more of 'everything's under control'?"

"Give me the witch's location," *Tauschung* ordered. The minion's eyes shot to the Power of Darkness. He nodded.

"Inside your dwelling. Actually"—the minion's face broke unexpectedly into a snaggle-toothed grin—"I think she's lost."

"Excellent," said *Tauschung*. "Things are proceeding just as I'd hoped. Now that she believes she stands a chance, her humiliation when she fails will be all the greater. All the more demoralizing. I'm sure I'll be able to end things in record time. Assuming there are no more interruptions."

"All right, all right. You've made your point," snarled the Power of Darkness. "Just make sure to bring me the betrayer's head."

"It will be a pleasure," said *Tauschung*, smiling.

Chapter
19

Cole jogged through the meadow. The muscles in his neck stood out in cords with the effort he was making not to look back over his shoulder. The area right between his shoulder blades burned with a constant itch. Moving through the open was hardly on Cole's list of top-ten ways to travel through demon territory. He might as well paint a target on his back and be done with it.

Still, if going through the open was the only way to get to Phoebe, then that's what Cole would do.

It didn't mean he had to like it.

As he jogged, he kept his senses on full alert. Ears cocked for the slightest unusual sound. His eyes darting from side to side, to take in as much of the territory around him as possible. Territory he was all but certain belonged to *Tauschung*.

Cole could feel his heart rate kick up as he

continued to jog. He was moving up a rise. The itch between his shoulder blades intensified. On instinct, Cole dropped to his belly, then continued to move commando-style. It took a little longer, but it definitely cut down on his overall visibility.

Cole reached the top of the rise and eased his head up over the crest. Before him, the land dipped down, then rose again, sharply. At the top of a big hill sat what Cole could only describe as a castle.

No, a château, he corrected himself. That's what an aristocrat named Nicolas Gerrard would have called it. *Looks like I've come to the right place*, Cole thought. Silently, he gave a mental thumbs-up to Charon.

Though every sense Cole had was screaming at him to hurry, he stayed right where he was. Rushing in without thought would be the demon thing to do. But Cole was human now. He might not be able to out-zap his foes, but he was pretty sure he could out-think them. It was strategy, not brute force, that would win Cole the day.

He lowered his head—there was no sense in presenting a target when he didn't absolutely have to—and considered the situation, running options and scenarios in his mind.

If Cole left out the rather unusual way he'd crossed the Boundary, discovering Phoebe's whereabouts had been pretty darned straightforward, even with the help he'd received from

Charon. Add to that the fact that Cole hadn't
been attacked since entering the underworld,
and the math really only added up to one thing:
Cole was right where *Tauschung* wanted him. A
thing that reinforced Cole's read on the situation, though it didn't free Phoebe. Yet.

Obviously, the next step was to get into the
château. The question was, how should Cole go
about it? He could hardly just walk right up to
the front door and knock. *Or can I?* he wondered
suddenly. Hadn't he just decided that finding
the château was exactly what *Tauschung* wanted? Couldn't that also mean that *Tauschung*
wanted Cole to get inside?

The ease with which Cole had located the
château could just be a tease, of course. Bait to
dangle in front of him before he was wiped out.
But somehow, Cole didn't think so. From what
he'd seen of him so far, *Tauschung* preferred the
up-close-and-personal approach. He'd want to
take Cole down himself. That meant he had to
let Cole in, a thing that just happened to fit
Cole's own plan rather nicely.

Besides, *Tauschung* had in his possession a
much better bait than reaching the château. He
had what was inside it: Phoebe, herself.

Satisfied with his read on the situation, Cole
stood up, target or not. *It's showtime,* he thought.
Tauschung wanted up close and personal, up
close and personal was what he'd get.

Fearlessly now, Cole strode down the slope

toward the château. The place that would be the scene of the final showdown between the demon who had become a man, and the man who'd pledged himself to a demon.

Cold in his gut, as Cole's long legs ate up the ground, was the knowledge that only one of them would make it out alive.

Chapter
20

Phoebe crept down the corridor, trying to keep her frustration from tearing her apart. Nick's château might be his palace. It was also one heck of a maze, Phoebe thought. She'd been creeping steadily along for what felt like hours, trying to find the way out. As far as she could tell, all she'd done was go around in circles.

Something was going to have to give. Phoebe, or the château.

She passed a tapestry of a stag being torn apart by a pack of dogs. For a split second, Phoebe paused. Hadn't she gone by a tapestry just like that, a few turns back? No, she decided. That tapestry had depicted a fox being torn apart by a pack of hounds. Plainly, Nick was big on art that featured hunters versus prey. With predictable results.

Get a grip, Halliwell, Phoebe chastised herself

as she began to move once more. So she was having a little trouble. That was to be expected. She was in the enemy's stronghold. It was hardly likely they'd make things easy on her. Besides, if the images *Tauschung* had revealed earlier were anything to go by, the environment through which Phoebe was moving was a whole lot more comfortable than where Cole was.

Cole. Sweetheart. Where are you right now? she thought. She reached an intersection and selected the right-hand passage this time. On the stone wall beside her, one of the burning torches that illuminated the corridors of the château revealed yet another tapestry. Phoebe ignored it.

The truth was, Cole could be dead now, and Phoebe would never know it. *No! That's not true!* she thought as she abruptly stopped walking. If Cole had lost his life, she would feel it. They were too closely connected for her not to.

Can you feel me, Cole? she thought, as she resumed walking. *Do you know I'm free? Well, almost free. Do you know I'm trying to find you?*

She turned another corner and walked straight into his arms.

"*Cole!*" Phoebe cried. "Thank goodness I've found you. Thank goodness you're all right."

"Sshh, Phoebe. It's okay," Cole said. As his strong arms came around her, Phoebe felt herself engulfed by a myriad of emotions so powerful, they left her shaken. Rage. Fear. Triumph. Longing. She was uncertain if what she felt emanated from her own heart, or from the one of the man who held her.

Phoebe eased back, looking up into Cole's face. "How did you find me?" she asked.

Cole snorted as he began to urge her along the corridor at a rapid pace. "Actually, it was pretty straightforward. Old *Tauschung*'s not as smart as he thinks he is."

"I know," Phoebe said as she hurried along. "Actually, I feel kind of sorry for him."

Cole stopped so abruptly, Phoebe skidded into him. "*Sorry* for him? He tricks you into the underworld, threatens your life and mine, and you feel sorry for him?"

"He's been hurt," Phoebe said, stung by Cole's tone into defending her reaction to *Tauschung*. "He made the wrong choice, and now it's trapped him, though I don't think he knows it. It doesn't make me want to be on his side or anything, but yes, I do feel sorry for him."

Cole's eyes narrowed dangerously. "Sounds like the two of you have gotten to know each other pretty well. Tell me something, Phoebe. Did I just come all this way and risk my life for nothing?"

Phoebe's breath caught in her throat. Ever so slowly, she took one step back, then another. Putting herself out of arm's reach. "You're not Cole. You're *Tauschung*."

The thing wearing Cole's face laughed, and then its features began to alter. For a moment, the sequence was a repeat of what Phoebe'd witnessed before, when she'd tried to goad *Tauschung* into revealing what he truly looked like. The features began to blur, as if folding in on one another. Then, as Phoebe watched, Nick's face slowly emerged, replacing Cole's. The contemporary dress stayed the same, Phoebe noticed. Probably because it would be easier to fight in, she thought.

"Very good," Nick said. "I wondered how long it would take you to catch on."

"How'd I do?" Phoebe asked through clenched teeth.

Nick consulted a watch. "Just a little under two minutes," he said. "Faster than I'd anticipated, I'll give you that. Tell me, Phoebe. What tipped you off?"

"Your attitude," Phoebe said, seeing no reason not to be honest. "Cole wouldn't have wondered if he'd risked his life for nothing. And he never would have thought I'd spend my time down here cozying up to you. He knows he can trust me."

Nick's eyebrows rose. "Oh, really," he said. "It didn't look that way the other night."

"That was then, this is now," Phoebe said, simply but forcefully. "Humans may make mistakes, but Cole is one guy who doesn't make the same mistake twice."

"You seem awfully sure of that," Nick said.

"That would be because I am."

"And are you as certain you can trust yourself?"

"What the heck is that supposed to mean?" Phoebe demanded.

Nick grinned, then cocked his head, as if listening to something Phoebe couldn't hear. She felt a tingle of alarm slide down her spine. *He is definitely up to something*, she thought. Whatever had occurred in the interval since she'd seen him last, Nick had regained his balance. He was back in control, and Phoebe couldn't exactly say she liked it.

"Tell you what," Nick said. "Let's find out. Your opportunity is on its way. It should be here right about . . . *now!*"

Phoebe made a lightning-fast connection. "Cole! Look out!" she shouted, just as Cole himself came barreling around the corner.

"Run, Phoebe," he commanded. Then, without hesitation, Cole flung himself at *Tauschung*.

Before Phoebe could even reject Cole's suggestion—she was hardly about to run away and leave him to fight alone—two demon minions stepped up behind her and seized her by both arms. Phoebe struggled, but it was useless. She was a good fighter, but the truth was, the demons had taken her completely by surprise. *Tauschung* had been pretty much a one-on-one kind of guy until that point.

He isn't taking any chances, Phoebe thought. *He means to win, no matter what.* Frustrated, feeling furious with herself and helpless, she stood and watched the battle between Cole and *Tauschung* unfold.

Tauschung absorbed Cole's rush by going down, tossing Cole over his head as he rolled onto his back. Cole flipped over in midair, came down on his feet, then spun around, already moving into a battle crouch. *Tauschung*, Nick, assumed the same position. For the space of several racing heartbeats, the two adversaries stared at each other.

How alike they look, Phoebe thought. *Like two sides of the same coin.* Opposite, yet connected.

"Still trying to play the hero, aren't you?" Nick taunted, as he and Cole began to circle around each other. "She isn't worth it, you know."

"Save it," Cole said. "And, for the record, in my experience, being the good guy is a whole lot more satisfying than being the bad guy."

Nick gave a short laugh. "Only because you've got it wrong."

"I don't think so." Cole made a sudden feint to the left. Instantly, Nick countered. *They're testing each other,* Phoebe realized, recognizing the techniques that Cole had taught her. Each was looking for a weakness in the other before the true battle began.

As far as Phoebe could see, Cole and Nick were almost perfectly matched. *What will tip the scales?* she wondered. *The power of love, or the power of pain? Which will prove to be the stronger?*

"So," Cole said as he countered a move from Nick. "What's it going to be, Gerrard? Do we stand around talking all day, or do we get down to business?"

Nick grinned. "I thought you'd never ask."

He launched himself straight at Cole, changing even as Cole tried to counter. In horror, Phoebe watched as Nick's body metamorphosed into something no longer human, a thing straight out of a late-night horror film. A thing with a thick, powerful body and long, grasping arms. They were twice as long as a man's. They ended not in hands, but in enormous hooked claws.

The demons holding Phoebe hooted in appreciation as the claws swung out at Cole, literally whistling through the air. At the last possible instant, Cole danced aside. With a horrible *smack*, the claws connected with the wall. *Tauschung* gave a howl of pain as chips of stone rained down.

Before *Tauschung* could change form again, Cole gave a roar, put his head down, and charged.

His head connected solidly with *Tauschung*'s midriff. The two went staggering back. Cole wrapped his arms around his adversary's body, staying in close, trying to minimize the fighting power of the long arms and hooked claws. Then, to Phoebe's dismay, *Tauschung* began to change again, his body becoming long and sinuous as a snake's. He slipped from Cole's grasp, slid to the floor, then darted behind him. Cole whirled around, once more assuming his battle crouch. *Tauschung* rose up to face him. As he did so, he resumed a human form.

Better, but still not good, Phoebe thought.

If she'd encountered this guy on the street, she'd have crossed it to avoid him. Big and beefy, *Tauschung's* newly chosen human body strained against the seams of his clothes. His eyes were bloodshot, narrowed with an animal cunning. He looked like a Neanderthal on steroids. Yet he moved toward Cole as nimbly as a dancer, his fists up to protect his face. Behind them, his lips curled in a taunting smile.

"Fighting as something more-than-human seems so unfair," *Tauschung* said as one fist shot out with the force of a projectile weapon. The powerful blow missed Cole's face by half an inch. The opponents pivoted, then faced each other again. *Tauschung* bouncing up and down on the balls of his feet like a boxer. Cole, swaying from side to side, staying low.

"A more human *touch*," *Tauschung* said with a grunt, his fist flashed out again. Again, at the very last moment, Cole managed to avoid it. "A more human touch just seems more personal, wouldn't you say?"

"I'd say you talk too much," said Cole.

Tauschung laughed, a sound that raised goose bumps on Phoebe's arms.

"Okay. I'll stop," he said, his tone agreeable. "I'd rather tear you to pieces anyhow."

Before he'd even finished speaking, *Tauschung* lashed out again, his right fist shooting forward, just as it had done twice before. But this time, as Cole countered left, *Tauschung*'s other fist suddenly hurtled out in a brutal blur of motion.

Phoebe heard the distinctive *splat* of flesh connecting with flesh. A crunch she feared was bones being broken. Cole's head snapped back like a rag doll's, blood streaming down his face. At the sight of it, the demons holding Phoebe began to shriek in approval and delight, but their hold on her arms never faltered.

Cole reeled back several steps, then righted himself. Phoebe tensed, expecting *Tauschung* to close in again at once, to try to finish what he had started. But, to her astonishment, he danced away. *He wants to prolong this, to toy with Cole,* she thought. An insight that seemed borne out by *Tauschung*'s next words.

"You didn't really think you could be a match for me, did you?" he inquired as he darted in for a second blow. Cole blocked it with his arm, then landed a solid punch to *Tauschung*'s stomach. Quickly, he followed up with another. *Tauschung* grunted, then danced away once more.

Good for you, Cole, Phoebe thought. But even she could see that Cole's blows had little effect. It was sort of like punching a telephone pole. Cole was the best fighter she knew, on a number of levels. He was well-trained. Disciplined. Fast and strong. But the bitter truth was that, no matter what his training, Cole was no physical match for the form *Tauschung* had assumed. Phoebe doubted any ordinary mortal was.

That would be the point, she thought. It was part of the lesson *Tauschung* was desperate to teach. That he'd made the right choice, while Cole had not.

"How long do you think you'll be able to keep this up?" *Tauschung* inquired as he danced close to Cole once more. "Sooner or later, you're going to tire. Sooner, probably."

In an unexpected blur of motion, he whirled and leaped, kicking out like a kung fu expert, planting one foot solidly in Cole's gut. Cole grunted as the air was forced from his lungs. But his reaction time was still quick. Almost as soon as the blow had landed, he was reaching for *Tauschung*'s ankle, twisting viciously. Again, *Tauschung* used the momentum of Cole's attack against him, flowing into Cole's own motion.

As Phoebe watched, *Tauschung*'s form abruptly grew smaller, arms folded across his chest, held tight into his body. He twisted like a figure skater, his body fully extended in a position no figure skater had ever managed: horizontal. As he landed on his feet he resumed his former, enormous body, then danced out of range again.

"You see the problem, don't you?" he went on. *He isn't even winded*, Phoebe thought. Fit as he was, Cole was sucking air, still recovering from the force of *Tauschung*'s blow.

"You have only one form, a form that can only take so much. But I have endless possibilities. If one tires or is injured, I can simply choose another."

As if to prove his point, *Tauschung*'s body now began to change endlessly, a seamless flow of motion. It reminded Phoebe of those commercials where the background stayed the same, but the person advertising the product altered constantly. There was no way to even keep track of the number of shapes *Tauschung* assumed, there were so many of them.

Finally, the flow of movement stopped. Nick Gerrard and Cole Turner faced each other.

"Why don't you just give up now?" Nick asked softly. No longer taunting, now his voice was simple and sincere, as if he had suddenly become Cole's best friend. As if he wanted Cole to trust him.

"I promise to give you a quick, easy death, rather than a slow and painful one. You don't want Phoebe to watch you suffer, do you? You'd like to spare her, at least."

"Spare me," Cole suggested, in a waspish play on words.

Nick laughed. "Clever to the last, I see. But out of the question, unfortunately. Your life for my freedom. I'm afraid it's a necessary part of my bargain."

"So that's what this is really all about," Cole

said. "Trying to change the bargain. Don't tell me being illusion-boy has lost its charm."

Nick laughed again. "Hardly. But being a minion definitely has. I kill you, my powers are my own, forever. Not even the Power of Darkness can take them from me."

"You don't actually believe he'll keep that bargain, do you?" Cole asked.

"Actually, I do," Nick answered. "You should consider it a compliment. It's a measure of how badly he wants you dead."

"Keep talking and you may just bore me to death," Cole remarked.

"You want to end this quickly? Fine by me. To tell you the truth, you were starting to get on my nerves, anyhow."

"No!" Phoebe cried out. She tried to throw herself forward. The demons yanked her back, the rough scales on their hands digging into her arms.

But it was too late. Nick and Cole were already hurtling toward each other, then locked in mortal combat.

Chapter
21

"I'm putting a stop to this," Paige said. "Right now."

In the attic at Halliwell Manor, Piper gave an anguished moan. Blood welled from her mouth and nose.

The final battle between Cole and *Tauschung* had gone deadly for Cole so quickly, there'd been no time for Paige to put her rescue plans into effect before Piper had suffered damage as well. The link between Piper and Cole established by the scrying spell was very plainly still in effect.

"Be careful, Paige," Leo warned. "You've seen how powerful *Tauschung* is. If he gets in even one blow—"

"I'll just have to make sure that doesn't happen," Paige replied, her tone determined. She took a last look into the scrying bowl, fixing the details of Phoebe and Cole's location in her mind.

"Okay," she said, pulling in a deep breath. Her eyes focused on Leo's concerned ones, for just an instant. "Here's to the element of surprise."

Summoning all her strength, Paige began to orb. She could feel the tingling sensation that always seemed to accompany the process flood through her body, increasing in intensity until Paige felt as if she were standing in the middle of an electrical storm. Never had she felt the sensation so strongly. It was almost painful.

It must be because of where I'm trying to go, she thought. *Hold on, Phoebe. Hold on, Cole. I'm coming.*

The familiar surroundings of Halliwell Manor winked out abruptly. In the next instant, agonizing pain seared through Paige's body. It felt for all the world as if she'd slammed straight into a brick wall. The next thing she knew, she was lying flat on her back on the attic floor.

"*No!*" she moaned. She struggled to rise to her feet. Her body felt bruised all over.

"What happened?" Leo asked, his tone urgent.

"I'm not sure," Paige acknowledged. "One minute, everything was fine. The next, it felt as if I'd literally hit a wall. Then, I ended up back here."

"I think you just had a close encounter with the barrier that separates the underworld from the world above," Leo said. "You'd have to pass through it to reach Phoebe and Cole. It takes a lot of energy, both psychic and physical. Believe me, I know."

"From when you went there before," Paige said, even though she knew she was stating the obvious.

Leo nodded. "Looks like I'm going back," he said. He started to rise.

"No, Leo, you can't!" Paige insisted. Swiftly, she moved to his side, urging him to maintain his position beside Piper.

"We went over this before. It's too risky. Besides, I don't think you can leave Piper. If you do . . ."

Paige's voice trailed off.

"Then we've lost Phoebe and Cole," Leo said simply. From beside him on the floor, Piper gave a low moan. Her breathing began to change, moving in and out of her body with a strange, liquid sound.

"Not yet we haven't," Paige declared. "There must be something we can do."

She began to move around the room, as if forcing her body into action might also force her desperate brain to come up with something. "If only we had a direct link," she said.

"Actually, I think we do," Leo said. "There's Piper's scrying spell."

Paige whirled suddenly, heading for the table where the bowl of water still showed Phoebe and Cole's location.

"The water!" she cried. From the floor beside Leo, Piper gave another moan.

"What are you thinking?" Leo asked. "Tell me."

"I can't touch the water because it will break the scrying spell, right?" Paige asked.

Leo nodded.

"But that might be a good thing," Paige went on. "It might help Piper. It would mean she'd no longer experience Cole's injuries."

"But we'd lose Phoebe and Cole for sure that way," Leo objected.

"Not necessarily," Paige said. "Not if I perform another spell."

There was a beat while Leo took in this new possibility. Then he nodded.

"Go for it."

Paige turned to the scrying bowl. She tried not to focus on the images she could see there. Cole, bleeding on the floor. Phoebe struggling with the demons that held her, desperate to get to him. *Tauschung*, the handsome face he'd chosen twisted in triumph. Then, even as Paige watched, the images began to dim.

I'm running out of time, she thought. *Tauschung's* master wanted to be in on the kill.

The Power of Darkness was coming.

Paige pulled in one deep breath to steady her nerves. Then, she began to recite her summoning spell.

● ● ●

Chapter
22

"Phoebe," Cole choked out.

With a sudden wrench, Phoebe freed herself from the grip of *Tauschung*'s demon minions. This time, he did nothing to prevent it. Phoebe hurried to Cole's side.

"Don't try to talk," she said as she knelt down beside him. "Save your strength. We're together. That's what matters. You did it. You found me, Cole."

"Love . . . Paige," Cole managed.

"I know. I love Paige too," Phoebe soothed. *Oh, God*, she thought. *He's not making any sense*. The end must be very close now.

"Well, Cole?" Nick said. "Still think it's better to be a good guy than a bad one? Guess you forgot that nice guys finish last. Thanks for giving me the opportunity to remind you."

Without warning, the torches illuminating the corridor flickered. Half of them went out.

Oh no, Phoebe thought. She had a feeling that could mean only one thing.

"Excellent," Nick said, confirming her worst fears. "My master is coming. I had a feeling he'd want to be in on this. At which point, he won't *be* my master any longer."

The lights flickered again. There was only one torch burning now, the one right above Phoebe and Cole. It was still enough for Phoebe to see Nick Gerrard's face. *How could I have ever thought he was handsome?* she wondered. In the harsh light of the underworld, Nick's face looked selfish and cruel.

"I'm about to have everything I've ever wanted, Phoebe," he said. "Do you have any idea what that feels like? I suppose I should thank you. After all, you helped make it possible. If you hadn't been so gullible, none of this would have happened."

"So human, you mean," Phoebe said as she tightened her grip on Cole. She knew Nick was talking as much about him as he was about her. "No matter what happens, I'd still rather be what I am than what you are."

"You mean dead?" Nick asked, just as the torch above Phoebe's head began to flicker wildly. A horrible coldness seemed to seep down the corridor.

"Phoebe," she heard Cole's voice gasp out. "I love you."

"I love you, too, Cole," Phoebe said.

"Now that," Nick put in, "is what I call touching. I can't wait to see what the two of you will do next."

As if his words had been a cue, light flooded through the corridor. Phoebe heard Nick give a shout of fury and dismay. Then the brightness around her became so dazzling, Phoebe did the only thing she could.

She held on to Cole with every ounce of strength she possessed, and closed her eyes.

Chapter
23

When she opened them again, she was sitting on the floor in the attic of Halliwell Manor, still cradling Cole in her arms. Leo was already moving toward them. Paige sat beside a small table. In her arms, she supported an unconscious Piper.

"Paige," Phoebe choked out. "Piper, what—"

"Don't worry," Paige reassured her. "As soon as Leo heals Cole, Piper will be all right. The scrying spell linked them together a little more strongly than we'd figured."

Anxiously, Phoebe watched as Leo laid a hand on Cole's chest, right over his heart. The other, he placed on the top of his head. Leo closed his eyes. Phoebe could see his healing Whitelighter energy flowing into Cole's body.

Please, she prayed silently. *Let Leo's healing powers be enough. Let him be in time.* If not, she might lose both another sister and the man she loved.

Cole's ordeal would have been for nothing. The Power of Darkness would win after all.

After a few tense moments, Leo leaned back. Cole drew in a deep breath and opened his eyes. Instantly, they locked onto Phoebe's. For a long moment, neither spoke.

"Hi," Cole finally said.

"Hi."

"So, I guess we made it back, huh?"

"Looks like it," Phoebe told him.

Slowly, Cole's eyes tracked around the room till they found Paige. "What's the matter with Piper?"

"Nothing," Piper herself answered as she sat up straight. "But that's the last underworld scrying spell I do for a while."

Leo got to his feet, then extended a hand to Cole. "Take it slow," he said as he eased him to his feet.

"Thanks," Cole said. His eyes met Leo's, then Paige and Piper's, in turn. "I mean it. Thanks a lot."

"Don't mention it," Piper said. "Though, if you felt like springing for a pizza, I wouldn't complain. I don't know about anyone else, but I'm starving."

"Half extra pepperoni, half the works?" Cole asked.

"No way," Paige put in. "I'm thinking one of each."

Cole laughed. Phoebe thought it was the best sound she'd ever heard.

"Okay," he said. "You've got a deal." His eyes sought Phoebe's as he moved to her and carefully pulled her into his arms. Phoebe laid her head against Cole's chest. She could hear his heart beat, sure and strong.

He was alive and well. They were together. She really did like happily ever after endings.

"If there's one thing I've learned about this family," Cole murmured for Phoebe's ears alone, "it's that you know how to drive a seriously hard bargain."

Chapter

24

Several hours later, the family was reassembled in the living room, stuffed full of pizza and salad. The ill effects from her exceptionally strong link with Cole over and done with, Piper had revived and whipped up a quick celebrational batch of brownies. The smell of them wafted through the room.

Leo had already tried to sneak one. Piper had caught him. To keep him away from them, she'd been forced to sit in his lap to hold him down. Cole and Phoebe snuggled together in front of the fireplace. Paige laid claim to the entire couch.

"So, what do you figure finally happened to *Tauschung*?" Paige asked.

"He lost," Phoebe said simply. "We won. My guess is that it had typical underworld-type results."

"So he got what was coming to him," Paige said.

"I think we can figure he did," Cole said. "Forgiveness isn't really an attribute of the Powers of Darkness."

Paige's glance slid to Piper. "Speaking of forgiveness," she said, "there's something Piper and I want to come clean about."

Phoebe's puzzled gaze moved from one sister to the other. "You want me to forgive you for being brilliant under pressure and rescuing us?" she asked.

"That, you may thank us for," Piper said as she climbed off Leo's lap to stand at Paige's side. "But I think she means something that happened before all that. Yes, Leo, you may now have a brownie, by the way."

Leo grinned on his way to the brownie pan. "I just love it when she makes it sound like I'm a twelve-year-old."

"Cut one for me, too," Cole requested. "A big one. I think we're about to have a Halliwell moment."

Phoebe gave him a playful sock in the shoulder. "Be quiet." She regarded her two sisters thoughtfully. "This is about how weird you guys have been behaving, isn't it?" she said. "I *knew* you were up to something."

Paige made a face. "We just wanted to give you a surprise. We'd have gone out to dinner if we'd have known you were going to eat with a major underworld figure instead."

"Okay, so, spill it," Phoebe said. "What's the big, bad secret?"

Paige and Piper exchanged a look, then spoke together.

"We booked you a day at your favorite spa."

"*What?*" Phoebe cried.

"You know—to pamper yourself before the wedding. It's sort of instead of a wedding shower," Piper explained.

"We wanted to make sure your favorite was the very best, so we had to do some research," Paige went on. "But every time we tried to discuss what we'd found out, you'd show up and we'd have to stop."

Phoebe shook her head in disbelief. "This will teach me not to jump to conclusions," she said. "Every time I came in and you guys stopped talking, I figured you were talking about me and Cole, and someone wasn't happy about us. Him. You know."

Cole sat up straight. "Hey, wait a minute," he protested.

"We *are* happy," Piper said. "You are our sister, and we love you. And Cole." She glanced at Paige.

"And we trust your decisions," Paige put in.

Phoebe felt a warm glow spread through her system. "That's what it all comes down to, isn't it? Trust."

"I'm really glad to hear you say that," Paige said. "Does this mean I can have the SUV whenever I want?"

The room erupted in a roar of laughter as the last of the tension brought on by their experiences slipped away.

"On two conditions," Phoebe said.

"What?" Paige asked.

"That I get a bigger brownie than Cole just had," Phoebe said. "And that you and Piper come with me to the spa."

"Done!" Paige said. She whisked the plate of brownies off the table and handed them to Phoebe. "How's that for size?"

"Hey, I didn't get any," Piper protested.

"Oops," Paige said. "Now that you mention it, neither did I!"

"Fortunately, I am prepared to share," Phoebe said. "After all, what are sisters for?"

**As many as one in three Americans with HIV...
DO NOT KNOW IT.**

**More than half of those who will get HIV this year...
ARE UNDER 25.**

**HIV is preventable.
You can help fight AIDS.
Get informed. Get the facts.**

**www.knowhivaids.org
1-866-344-KNOW**

. . . A GIRL BORN
WITHOUT THE FEAR GENE

FEARLESS™

A SERIES BY
FRANCINE PASCAL

PUBLISHED BY SIMON & SCHUSTER

3029-01

• • • • • • • • • • • •

When I was six months old, I dropped from the sky—the lone survivor of a deadly Japanese plane crash. The newspapers named me Heaven. I was adopted by a wealthy family in Tokyo, pampered, and protected. For nineteen years, I thought I was lucky.
I'm learning how wrong I was.

I've lost the person I love most.
I've begun to uncover the truth about my family.
Now I'm being hunted. I must fight back, or die.
The old Heaven is gone.

I AM SAMURAI GIRL.

• • • • • • • • • • • •

A new series from Simon Pulse

The Book of the Sword
The Book of the Shadow

BY CARRIE ASAI

Available in bookstores now